"Talk to me, Sammie. We've been through too much to let anything stand between us," Jake said.

When she didn't answer, he closed the distance between them, then raised his hand to her cheek and stroked it. "You've always been able to say exactly what you were thinking to me. What's changed?"

He was standing so close, she could feel the heat from his body. She wanted to tell him what she was feeling but she didn't dare. She wiped a tear away. "It must be my hormones again," she said. "Making me feel things—"

He cupped her face with his palm as he gazed into her eyes. "What kind of things?"

She wished he wouldn't turn tender on her. "Jake—" His black eyes locked on hers, impaled her. She almost shivered. "I care for you. More than I should. Not just as a friend anymore."

He looked surprised, then thoughtful, and moved until their bodies were nearly touching. "So what are we going to do about it?"

She lowered her gaze to his chest and whispered, "I don't know."

Jake crooked one finger and nudged her chin until she had to look into his eyes once more. "I think we should make the best of it."

Sammie barely had time to register the words before his lips descended. She knew she was in trouble the moment his mouth opened over hers. . . .

WHAT ARE *LOVESWEPT* ROMANCES?

They are stories of true romance and touching emotion. We believe those two very important ingredients are constants in our highly sensual and very believable stories in the LOVESWEPT line. Our goal is to give you, the reader, stories of consistently high quality that may sometimes make you laugh, sometimes make you cry, but are always fresh and creative and contain many delightful surprises within their pages.

Most romance fans read an enormous number of books. Those they truly love, they keep. Others may be traded with friends and soon forgotten. We hope that each LOVESWEPT romance will be a treasure—a "keeper." We will always try to publish

LOVE STORIES YOU'LL NEVER FORGET
BY AUTHORS YOU'LL ALWAYS REMEMBER

The Editors

Loveswept ® 719

THE COP AND THE MOTHER-TO-BE

CHARLOTTE HUGHES

BANTAM BOOKS
NEW YORK · TORONTO · LONDON · SYDNEY · AUCKLAND

THE COP AND THE MOTHER-TO-BE
A Bantam Book / December 1994

ISBN 0-553-44390-9

Published simultaneously in the United States and Canada

Bantam Books are published by Bantam Books, a division of Bantam Dou-
bleday Dell Publishing Group, Inc. Its trademark, consisting of the words
"Bantam Books" and the portrayal of a rooster, is Registered in U.S.
Patent and Trademark Office and in other countries. Marca Registrada.
Bantam Books, 1540 Broadway, New York, New York 10036.

PRINTED IN THE UNITED STATES OF AMERICA

OPM   0 9 8 7 6 5 4 3 2 1

PROLOGUE

Lieutenant Jake Flannery shivered as he climbed the concrete stairs to the second floor apartment, followed by a uniformed officer. He didn't know if he was trembling from the chill in the air or because he'd just lost a fellow officer or because he'd killed a man. Probably a combination of the three. He wasn't thinking straight. He knew he was in shock, knew he should have gone home like he'd been ordered. But he'd refused.

"I have to go to Nathan's wife," he'd told the captain. "I can't let a stranger tell her."

The sides of his jacket flapped as a breeze knifed through him. Jake could not remember when December in Atlanta had been so cold—or dismal.

He still couldn't believe the events that had occurred in the past hour. A drug bust gone wrong. Somebody inside had obviously been tipped off at the last minute. His narcotics unit, along with DEA officials, had stormed the house and discovered the dealers inside had enough ammo to supply a terrorist group. The front man, in this case Nathan Webster, had received the full brunt of their firepower.

Jake paused before the door where a small welcome sign set it apart from the others. As though searching for strength, he glanced over his shoulder at the other officer. The man's face was chalky, his eyes rimmed with anguish. Jake knew he didn't look any better. Fifteen years on the force had not prepared him for this. For losing one of his own. For having to break the news to the wife.

He raised his hand to knock.

Samantha Webster checked the roast and saw that it still needed a good half hour. Perfect. That would give her and Nathan time to have a drink in front of the fireplace. She glanced toward the living room and saw the fire was burning brightly. A rather forlorn Scottish pine stood in one corner, waiting to be decorated. Perhaps tonight. Perhaps it was going to be a wonderful Christmas after all—once she told him. "I have wonderful news, Nathan," she'd say.

She frowned suddenly. Unless, of course, he brought company home with him, which was often the case. Jake Flannery. Then she'd have to postpone the news. She made a small sound of irritation. She knew Nathan idolized his boss, but that didn't mean he had to invite the man in every night. It irritated her further because Nathan had absolutely no business hanging out with a single guy, especially one with Jake Flannery's reputation. Nathan refused to listen. As far as he was concerned, they didn't make 'em any better than Jake.

Someone knocked on the door, startling her from her thoughts. Had Nathan forgotten his key again? He could be scatterbrained at times. He'd only recently been promoted to the narcotics unit and that's all he thought about. He wanted to be a good cop, the best on the force. Like his daddy and his granddaddy before him.

She hurried across the room, unlocked the door and pulled it open, bringing with it the chill from outside. Her eyes did a double take when she found Jake standing on the other side.

"What are you doing here?" She noted the uniformed policeman behind him, and the look on Jake's face.

"There was a bust today, Sammie," he said, using the nickname Nathan had given her. "Something went wrong."

Her heart leapt to the back of her throat, her eyes registered fear. "Where's my husband?" she demanded.

"Honey, Nathan was shot."

She told herself to remain calm. He'd said shot, not killed. "Let me get my coat, and I'll go to the hospital with you."

Jake grabbed her wrist, bringing her to a halt. A pained expression crossed his face. "He didn't make it to the hospital."

It took a minute for his meaning to sink in. A tortured cry was torn from her lips. "No, Jake, don't you *dare* tell me that! No!"

He stepped closer, pushing her inside the apartment. The look in her eyes was wild. The uniformed officer followed them in, closed the door. Jake grasped her by the shoulders, wanting to calm her but didn't know what to say. What *could* he say? "Nathan was killed in the line of duty. He was very brave." It sounded lame even to his own ears.

"That's supposed to make me feel better?" she yelled, pounding on his chest. "Is it? How could you let this happen, Jake? You're supposed to be the best." She was so caught up in her pain, she couldn't see the lines of grief on his own face. She was sobbing now. "What about the baby?"

Jake heard her, but the words didn't register at first. "What are you talking about? *What* baby?"

She slumped against him, the thought of losing her husband being more than she could bear. "I'm pregnant," she managed, no longer taking pleasure in that fact.

ONE

Sammie Webster paused at her front door, a sack of groceries in each arm. In the parking lot below she heard a car door slam, and glanced over the railing where a big man with jet-black hair was climbing out of a fire engine-red Jeep Cherokee. Jake was early. He looked up, caught a glimpse of her standing there and raced up the stairs.

"What the hell are you doing?" he demanded, his dark face taking on a lethal frown she was certain had earned him his dangerous reputation. That, and the jagged scar along his jaw that had never healed properly. She'd heard it had come from a broken beer bottle. He took the bags from her arms. "You know you're not supposed to be carrying anything heavy."

She ignored him, digging through her purse for her keys. Although she was at least a foot shorter and weighed almost half as much as he, she wasn't the least bit intimidated by his gruff demeanor. She had seen another side of Jake Flannery these past six months.

". . . dangerous to stand outside your door digging for your keys?" he said. "How many times have I told you? That is how women get attacked."

Sammie turned to him and very calmly tucked a strand of reddish-blond hair behind one ear. She was wearing a tank-style trapeze dress that was meant to conceal her pregnancy and keep her cool in the June temperatures but did neither. Her green eyes were amused as they locked with his dark ones. "Are you going to act like this all evening?" she asked. "Because if you are, you can turn your butt around and forget dinner. Besides, I'm seven and a half months pregnant. I hardly think a man's going to lose his head."

"Rape has nothing to do with desire. It's an act of violence. We've been through this before."

"Yeah, yeah, yeah." She pushed her key into the lock and opened the door, then waited for him to get inside with the groceries before closing it.

"Lock it," he told her as he entered the cinnamon-scented apartment.

She rolled her eyes but obeyed anyway. "You'd think I lived in Beirut," she muttered, kicking her shoes off. "This happens to be a very nice neighborhood." She went into the kitchen.

"Sit," Jake said, pointing to a chair. "I'll unload the groceries."

"Yes, boss." Sammie lowered herself into a chair, thankful to be off her feet. She felt bigger than Mount Saint Helens, despite the fact she had kept her weight down so far. Except for that occasional binge. Cookies that she stuck in her freezer but discovered she could eat frozen if she craved them bad enough. Potato chips that she asked Jake to hide from her, only to spend the rest of the evening searching for them after he left. Why didn't she want to binge on green beans and tuna salad, she wondered.

She watched Jake shrug out of a navy jacket and drape it over the back of a chair. It was the only thing he wore that made him look even halfway respectable. The faded jeans, slightly wrinkled dress shirt, and grungy sneakers were more suited to a thug, not one of Atlanta's top plainclothes detectives. He pulled his holster off and placed it on top of the refrigerator. Just like Nathan used to do, she thought.

Jake opened the refrigerator and pulled out a beer. Sammie kept his brand on hand. He took a long swig, then stood there for a moment, working his shoulders and neck muscles, getting rid of the stresses of the day.

She watched him with growing fascination.

He was a big man, but graceful. Comfortable with his body. "Tough day?" she asked.

He shrugged. "Just busy." Jake glanced around the room as he spoke. He liked how she'd decorated the apartment. Although she'd had to get permission from the manager, Sammie had done away with the drab beige so often found in rental property. Her kitchen was painted a dark tangerine shade that set off the white cabinets. A floral border, matching curtains and chair cushions added the finishing touch. The rest of the place bore her personality as well. Sammie was the only woman he knew, including his mother, who used a sewing machine these days.

Jake sipped the rest of his beer while he unloaded the groceries. Her refrigerator sparkled as though it was brand-new. A large box of baking soda sat at the back, ready to absorb the first offensive odor, which he was certain had never found its way inside either the refrigerator or the apartment. So different from his own refrigerator. He didn't put food in there often enough to worry about keeping it clean. With everything stowed away, Jake closed the door and glanced at her sitting there barefoot. "Feet hurt?"

She nodded. "I guess I need bigger shoes, huh?"

He crossed the room, sat down before her Indian style and grabbed one foot. "What you need is one of Jake's famous foot massages," he said, squeezing the ball of her foot gently and working his way to her instep.

She squirmed through the first ticklish moments, but as he began to apply more pressure to her tired muscles, kneading away the soreness, she leaned back in the chair and gave in to the wonderful sensations. "Oh, that feels soooo good," she said, enjoying the tingling in her ankle and calf. His hands were big and warm. Comforting. She closed her eyes and relaxed. Her body became less taut, loose, as the warmth from his hands spread up her entire leg.

He changed to the other foot.

She opened her eyes and tried to stay alert. It wasn't easy. His touch lulled her into a sense of well-being.

"So what's new with you these days?" she asked, deciding conversation was a good way to stay awake. "How's your love life?" Now there was a subject unlikely to put her to sleep, she thought. His amorous adventures had been the topic of many of their conversations, but he told her only enough to make her curious for more.

He shrugged. "I can't complain. I was thinking about asking the new dispatcher out, but she's got an attitude."

"What kind of attitude?"

"Like she's the Queen of Sheba and the rest of us are hillbillies. I wouldn't take her to a hog-killin'."

"I give you twenty-four hours."

He glanced up. "For what?"

"Before you ask her out. Does she have children?"

"Better not."

"That's right, you don't like children and don't understand why they exist."

"So, I'm selfish."

"I don't think you're as selfish as you claim," she said, remembering how he'd been there for her when her dead husband's family had been unable to rise above their own grief to offer Sammie much comfort.

"Believe me. I've known myself for thirty-eight years, and I'm as selfish as they come." He was quiet for a moment as he rubbed and squeezed the soreness out of her foot. She had cute feet. Nice legs, too, although he was certain she'd flip out if he told her so. She didn't expect him to notice things like that any more than he expected her to notice he'd had his hair trimmed or was wearing a new shirt. "So how's the pet store and grooming business?" he asked, keeping the conversation safe.

"Busy. I'm interviewing groomers so I'll have someone to take my place once the baby comes. She paused as he wiggled her toes. "You working on anything new?"

"Yes, but I'm not telling you."

"Why not? I tell you about my job."

" 'Cause you've got a mouth bigger than Texas and you'll repeat all this confidential, highly classified information I'm carrying around up here." He tapped the side of his head.

"I will not!" she said vehemently. "Besides, it can't be much. Not if you're storing it all up there."

He looked offended. "It's not wise to insult a man while he's holding your foot, Sammie." Jake closed his hand around one surprisingly trim ankle. She screamed before he even touched her with the other hand, obviously knowing what he was about to do.

"Please don't!" she begged.

He tickled her anyway.

She cried out and threatened to go into labor if he didn't stop.

The threat worked. His hands stilled immediately.

"Okay, I'll tell you what's going on at work if you promise to keep your mouth shut." She nodded and drew an imaginary X across her left breast. He watched her, intrigued with how her breasts had filled out these past six months. There was a soft roundness, a lushness that hadn't been there before.

"There's a gun-smuggling racket going on south of the city," he said, turning his thoughts away from her changing body. "We've only been watching them for a few days. It'll be interesting to see what happens."

Sammie was quiet for a minute. She raised

fearful eyes to his. "Guns, huh? You'll be careful?"

He gazed back at her, regretting that he'd said anything. He knew she was thinking of Nathan. She didn't seem to think about it all the time now like she used to, but he could tell it still crept up on her now and then. He smiled confidently and gave her foot one last squeeze. "I'm always careful, babe." He stood. "Now, what can I do to help with dinner?"

Sammie knew it was his way of bringing the topic to a close. That's the way Jake was. If she got him to discuss a case, any case, he told her very little. If she worried about his safety, he was quick to assure her but changed the subject before she could question him further. Did he think she was afraid that he was not capable of protecting himself and his men now that he'd lost Nathan?

She knew she would regret till the day she died those few seconds she'd blamed him for Nathan's death. She'd obviously been in shock at the time. She had apologized for it later but knew she would never be able to take the words back. Was that the reason Jake insisted on looking after her now, because he'd been unable to prevent her husband's death? He'd been having dinner with her on Thursday night for months. Unless something important came up, he didn't miss.

"You know what I think?" Jake said when she

didn't answer him right away. "I think we should start going out to dinner on Thursday night instead of you cooking. You need to get out more."

She realized she'd been staring into space. "What do you mean I need to get out? I'm out all day." She chuckled. "I suppose I could go to one of those singles' bars downtown. You know anybody looking for a fat lady?"

"You're not fat, you're pregnant. There's a difference."

She looked down at her protruding belly. "Not from where I'm sitting."

"Besides . . ." he grinned. "You're kind of cute that way. It looks like you've swallowed a watermelon."

She pursed her lips together and pointed to the living room. "Go watch TV, Jake. All this flattery might go to my head."

He grabbed his beer and started past her, then stepped back and kissed her on the forehead. "Let me know if there's something I can do to help, pudge."

She picked up a wet dishcloth and threw it at him, but he ducked and it hit the wall and slid to the floor.

"Training," he said smugly as he walked through the doorway. He paused and glanced over his shoulder. "I wish I could be a fly on the wall in here when you try to bend over and pick that up."

It wasn't until they had finished their dinner

—fettuccine Alfredo and Caesar salad—and Jake was enjoying a cup of mocha-almond coffee when Sammie brought up the topic that had been on her mind all day. "I need a favor, Flannery," she said.

"You got it, babe."

"I'd like for you to be my childbirth coach."

He arched one black brow. "Say what?"

"I've decided to take prepared childbirth classes. My doctor highly recommends them. They'll teach me breathing and relaxation techniques that are supposed to help me during labor and delivery."

"I thought that's what drugs were for."

"That's the way it used to be. Now they like to keep the mother alert."

His black eyes narrowed into a look of outright suspicion. "Wait a minute, I think I've heard of this," he said. "Is this where the guy gets stuck going into the delivery room?"

Her brow puckered in a frown. "Stuck? That's a unique word choice."

He ignored her. "Because if it is—" He paused. "I don't think so."

She saw the determined look in his eyes, the stubborn, almost rigid set of his square jaw, but she wasn't about to be deterred. "What are you afraid of?"

One would have thought she'd just accused him of bad hygiene. His expression changed to indignation. "I'm not *afraid* of anything."

"That's not what it sounds like to me," she said. She gave a snort and pushed her chair away from the table. "And Nathan said you were brave. Baloney!"

She was playing with his head. He stared at her for a moment, and she knew he was trying to think of a way to get out of what she was suggesting without turning her down flat. "Wouldn't you feel self-conscious having me in there? I mean, I've never even seen you in a bathing suit, much less a . . . you know . . . sheet."

"Why should I be embarrassed? You've been through the whole pregnancy with me. Remember in the beginning when I was sick to my stomach all the time? Who stood outside the bathroom door with a wet cloth? You're practically my best friend, Jake." He looked surprised but flattered. "I would never have made it without you these past months, you know that." She sometimes suspected he felt the same way about her—they'd grieved together over Nathan—but he would turn his gun on himself before admitting as much.

He gave her a knowing look. "You're desperate, aren't you? Otherwise, you wouldn't be saying these nice things to me. Did everybody else turn you down?"

"The only person I asked was Ruby from work. She didn't think she could do it. I thought of Nathan's mother, but she's still having a tough time of it." Sammie knew his parents had taken his death hard. They seldom left the house anymore. "I wanted to ask you from the very beginning, but I was afraid you'd feel uncomfortable." When he didn't say anything, she went on. "You might enjoy it, Jake. And there's no reason for either of us to feel self-conscious. Childbirth is a natural life process."

"If I do it, will you name the baby after me?" he said jokingly, trying to buy a little more time.

She laughed. "You know I've already picked out the names. If it's a boy, his name will be Nathan Daniel, and if it's a girl I'll name her Stephanie Marie."

"Just kidding," he said. He pondered it. Who else could she ask? She had no family. And they *were* good friends. Like she said, *best* friends. They'd been through a lot these past six months. He sighed heavily. "Well, since there's so much in it for me, I'll do it," he said, irritated that he hadn't been able to think of a way to get out of it. "But only because I know you'll hound me until I give in. Now I know why Nathan was so henpecked."

"Nathan was *not* henpecked."

He ignored her. "And that's exactly why I don't get married. As soon as you women snare a man—"

"Snare, Jake? Did you say *snare*?"

"—you think you can tell him what to do for the rest of his sorry life."

Sammie merely smiled. "You just wait, Jake Flannery. One of these days you're going to fall hard for someone."

"When pigs fly."

"And she's going to put a ring through your nose and lead you around like a puppy dog." Sammie was thoughtful for a moment, and when she spoke again her tone was gentle.

"Nathan couldn't have been too henpecked," she said. "He became a cop, didn't he? Despite the fact that I was dead set against it."

It was nearing ten o'clock when Jake left Sammie's place after reminding her to lock up tight. He would have enjoyed staying longer, but after watching her yawn for the past twenty minutes, he decided she needed sleep more than company. He climbed in his Jeep and headed south on the interstate, toward the city. Maybe he'd stop by the Pit and have a drink with the guys. But he hadn't gone more than a couple of miles before he decided to head home instead. He was drained.

He was also down in the dumps. Spending time with Sammie sometimes did that to him. Not because he found her depressing to be around. She was anything but. She had bounced back from the tragedy better than he'd expected. Nevertheless, he felt sorry for her. Sorry that she was having to go through the pregnancy all alone, sorry that she had no family, and especially sorry that she had no husband.

It was all his fault.

He pulled into his driveway twenty minutes later and parked in front of a frame house with a porch running across the front and around the sides. He liked the neighborhood. It was upper middle class with neat lawns and flower beds, where children rode bicycles in the middle of the road and fathers played ball with their sons in the backyard. The place offered a feeling of normalcy. In his business, where people were routinely shot and mugged and heaven knows what else, he appreciated the order.

Jake walked to the door, unlocked it and stepped inside, his eyes automatically searching the shadows for any signs of an intruder. There were none. In the years he'd been there, he'd never had a break-in. Still, he always checked—habit. Just as he always checked behind the seats when he climbed in his Jeep, just as he chose to sit facing the door in a restaurant. He liked being prepared. But he'd been totally unprepared for Sammie's invitation that he help her in the delivery room.

The house was a welcoming sight to him, a place where he could unwind and say to hell with everything else. It was sparsely furnished and meticulous, and it looked nothing like it had in the beginning.

They'd called it a "handyman special," which

was the only reason he'd been able to afford it on a cop's salary. The mortgage company had foreclosed on the family who'd lived there prior, when the man had lost his job and hadn't been able to find another one. Before he left, he kicked holes in the walls, destroyed the carpeting and appliances, took a sledgehammer to the tile, and ran a bag of nails down the garbage disposal.

Jake had bought it at a bargain price but had been forced to live with the disrepair until he could afford to do something about it.

He put his holster on top of the refrigerator, opened it and pulled out a ginger ale, then carried it into the living room. He checked his messages and found nothing urgent. His remote control was on the arm of the sofa. He sat down, flipped the television on, then ran through a number of channels before settling on the sports station.

He drank the ginger ale and watched TV for a moment but soon lost interest.

Once again, he thought of Sammie. How could he not say yes? Another swig of soda. He had stomach problems, had had stomach problems ever since Nathan's death. Couldn't eat Mexican food anymore. Couldn't eat anything spicy for that matter, unless he was prepared to sit up half the night drinking ginger ale. He was going to end up just like his captain who made a steady diet of antacids.

Why had Sammie asked him to be her coach?

he wondered. Didn't she know what he'd gone through over her husband's death?

Jake allowed himself to think about it for once, instead of stuffing it into that part of his brain that held unpleasant memories, memories collected from fifteen years of police work. He took them out from time to time, examined them, relieved that some had grown fuzzy around the edges over the years. Those were the ones he had the least trouble letting go, like closing a file in his mind, tossing it out so there was less clutter.

He couldn't get rid of Nathan's file. It haunted him. Nathan Webster had been a hot-head who often acted and *then* asked questions. What he was doing on the police force, in narcotics, of all places, was beyond Jake. Other than the fact his whole family tree was littered with cops. Jake had gone to the captain and told him Nathan's head wasn't screwed on right, but the captain had reminded him that Nathan was only a rookie detective and it was up to Jake to work with him. It wasn't until the funeral that Jake discovered the captain was close friends with Nathan's father who'd since retired.

That was one way to keep your job, he supposed.

Still, he should have pressed the issue, told the captain about Nathan's erratic behavior, forced him to be evaluated. Something wasn't quite right. No cop liked being sent to the front of the line in a drug bust, but he or she did it because it went with the territory. Nathan, on the other hand, said it gave him a rush and volunteered to use the sledgehammer and be the first one in each time. In his overzealousness, he rushed, took chances.

Nathan had taken several shots in the chest and one in the head before Jake could get him out of the line of fire and empty his own gun into the shooter.

A fiasco and a tragedy. One of those times when everything that could possibly go wrong *had* gone wrong. He was responsible. How could Sammie expect him to help bring Nathan's child into the world when he'd been partially responsible for taking Nathan out?

TWO

The Curly Q Pet and Grooming Salon was located in a strip shopping center north of the city, tucked between a submarine sandwich shop and a dry cleaner offering specials on dress shirts. Sammie had opened the shop eight years prior, shortly before she and Nathan married and only months before he had decided to be a cop like the rest of his family. Luckily, the store had become successful right away; so successful, in fact, she'd been forced to hire someone to run the cash register while she worked in the back grooming dogs.

Her assistant, Ruby Johnson, was a plump retired schoolteacher who claimed she'd loved staying home tending her roses until her husband retired as well and almost drove her crazy. Sammie had hired her on the spot. Ruby was like the grandmother she'd never had and had been instrumental in her getting through the past six months. Now, as the white-headed woman pushed through the glass front door, holding a sack in one hand, Sammie was reminded once again how lucky she was to have her.

"Lunch is here," the woman announced. She smiled and hurried down the aisle past the bird cages—cockatiels, lovebirds, finches, parakeets—and stopped before the long counter where the cash register sat. They usually ate out front instead of going into the tiny kitchen in back. Otherwise, they spent most of their time running back and forth as customers came in the door.

Ruby dug into the sack. "Okay, I have one Italian sub with extra olives and pickles for you—" She paused and handed the wrapped sandwich to Sammie. "And one turkey and cheese on whole wheat for me."

Sammie eagerly accepted her lunch. "Thanks, Ruby. Here's your drink." She handed her one of the soft drinks she'd retrieved from the small refrigerator in back.

"Whew, what a morning!" the older woman exclaimed as she took a moment to catch her breath. "We haven't had five minutes to ourselves. How many left to clip?"

"Three. And nine on the books tomorrow."

Ruby looked concerned. "You're wearing your support hose today, I hope."

"Yes." Sammie unwrapped her sandwich and took a bite. They were silent for a moment, but she could sense Ruby's impatience. "Well, aren't you going to ask me what he said?"

"Not unless you want to tell me."

"He agreed to do it."

Ruby looked shocked. "No!"

"You owe me a quarter."

Ruby fished two dimes and a nickel out of her skirt pocket. "How'd you talk him into it?"

"Actually, it wasn't as hard as I thought. 'Course, he could very well change his mind before the first class."

Ruby shook her head. "He won't change his mind. From what I know of Jake Flannery, if he says he's going to do something, he does it. He may hate it, and he may make you feel like dirt for ever getting him involved, but he'll see it through till the miserable end."

"I hope you're right because there's nobody else I'd feel comfortable asking. You and Jake are the closest friends I have."

Ruby patted her hand. "I'm just sorry I couldn't be your partner," she said, "but I told you right up front that I wasn't cut out for that sort of thing. I'd panic or burst into tears during your first contraction, and they'd kick me out of the room."

"I understand, Ruby. I just hope Jake is able to remain calm and levelheaded throughout the whole thing."

"I'd think after fifteen years on the police force nothing would faze him." They chatted about the groomer Sammie had interviewed that morning. Ruby ate part of her sandwich. "You want the other half?" she asked. "I can't eat the whole thing."

Sammie shook her head. "I won't be able to eat for a week once I finish this."

As though suspecting Sammie might change her mind, Ruby left the sandwich sitting on the counter instead of putting it away. "You're really fond of him, aren't you?"

Sammie chewed and swallowed. "Who, Jake? Of course I am."

"Do you think anything could ever come of it?"

Sammie looked up. "You mean do I think we'd ever become romantically involved? Not a chance."

"You sound sure of it."

"I was widowed before my thirtieth birthday, remember? I refuse to go through that again. Besides, that's not the way it is between Jake and me."

"You'd make a lovely couple," Ruby said wistfully. "Him so big and dark, and you so fair and petite."

"I'm not petite anymore," Sammie said, patting her stomach. "Besides, I think Jake prefers bimbos. That way he doesn't have to put forth much effort in a relationship, and he can concentrate on the police force."

"What a terrible thing to say."

Sammie looked apologetic. "I know it is, but I can't think of one reason a woman should become involved with a cop. Not one."

"How about love?"

Sammie shook her head. "Not good enough. You can love a man in a business suit just as much as one who straps on a gun before leaving for work." She finished her sandwich and reached for Ruby's. "Did I tell you the wallpaper for the nursery came in yesterday?" she asked, changing the subject abruptly. She knew she sometimes came off sounding bitter, and poor Ruby, who was as softhearted as they came, didn't always understand.

As though sensing Sammie needed to get away from the cop issue, Ruby picked up the new thread of conversation quite easily. "How does it look?"

"Adorable. Clouds with tiny teddy bears peeking through. I'm going to pick up the crib on the way home tonight. I might even start putting it together if I'm not too tired." She was prevented from saying more when the bell on the door tinkled, and a tall man in shorts and T-shirt walked in.

"I saw your sign out front about the kittens?"

"Oh, yes," Ruby said. "They're over there by the window. I'll be glad to help you." She glanced at Sammie. "Looks like our break is over."

Sammie nodded as she wadded up her trash

and tossed it in the garbage can below the counter. "Looks that way. Well, I've got dogs to clip." She went around the counter and made her way to the back as Ruby hurried toward the customer.

Sammie was more than a little tired when she finished for the day, but she made herself drive by the catalog store for the crib she'd ordered. Once a stockroom attendant loaded it into the trunk of her car, she drove straight home, looking forward to the moment when she could step out of her shoes and slip into something more comfortable. She parked in her usual spot, climbed out of the car, and opened the trunk. She tugged the box containing the crib and knew right away she'd never get it up two flights of stairs.

Damn!

Sammie gave a tired sigh. She hated having these limitations set on her. For as long as she could remember, she'd always done exactly *what* she wanted *when* she wanted. Perhaps it was because she'd grown up without family. Living with foster parents had forced her to become independent at an early age. Not because they were cruel or neglectful, which they weren't, but because Sammie felt they preferred doing things for their natural children. She had taught herself not to need anyone or anything. Nathan once told her that her tough exterior wasn't always flattering.

"Need a hand, Mrs. Webster?" a voice said.

Sammie jumped and turned around to find her neighbor's fifteen-year-old son standing only inches away. "Oh, Doug, I didn't hear you come up." She smiled. She liked the boy, mainly because of his red hair and an abundance of copper-colored freckles. She'd looked much the same growing up. Luckily, her hair had lightened and some of the freckles had faded over the years. "How'd you like to make a couple of bucks?" she said.

Doug carried the box up the stairs with very little effort, then waited until Sammie unlocked the door so he could take it inside. "Which room you want it in?" he asked.

"This way." She led him to one side of the apartment. The two bedrooms and their adjoining baths were located on opposite sides of the living room. This worried Sammie because she didn't like the idea of the baby sleeping that far away. Of course, he or she would sleep in the bassinet in Sammie's room in the beginning so the matter wasn't urgent. Perhaps after a few months she'd feel more comfortable with the situation if she used a monitor. "Just put it down right there," she said, already fumbling in her purse for the money.

The boy looked embarrassed when she offered it. "You don't really have to pay me, Mrs. Webster. I did it 'cause I wanted to."

"Nonsense, you earned it." She put two bills in his palm and closed his fist around it.

"You seen Jake lately?" he asked as she walked him to the door.

She knew the boy, who hadn't seen his father in years, idolized Jake. They'd even played tennis a couple of times, although both claimed the other was a terrible player. "He stops in from time to time. I think you've been out with friends the past few times." She knew Doug had a new girlfriend. His mother had mentioned it in the laundry room recently.

"Will you tell him hello for me? He said he's going to put in a good word for me when I'm old enough to join the force."

She frowned. "I thought you were going to be a veterinarian."

He grinned. "After hearing about Jake's job I think I'd have more fun being a cop."

"Now, you listen to me, Douglas Brenner," Sammie said, pointing a finger at him. "There's a lot of sweet innocent animals running the streets today that need good care. They need *you*. Why on earth would you want to work with a bunch of homicidal maniacs and maybe get shot when you could do so much for animalkind?"

She didn't realize she was shouting.

Doug had a funny look on his face, as though he'd only just remembered that she'd lost her husband in the police force. "Uh, I gotta go,

Mrs. Webster," he said. "You let me know if there's anything else I can carry up for you."

Sammie watched him go, thinking how young he was, how innocent. Why did he want to lose all that? Why did he yearn to become a hardened man who was forced to deal with so much ugliness?

A man like Jake.

Sammie had not forgotten about her conversation with the boy when Jake called Sunday night to invite her to a movie. "Are you trying to convince Doug Brenner to join the police force?" she demanded with a fervor that surprised them both.

He was silent for a moment. He could hear the disapproval in her voice loud and clear. "I ran into him when I was taking out the trash a few weeks ago. He asked me a million questions, and I tried to answer a few of them. Why?"

"He's wanted to be a veterinarian all his life," she said. "His mother and his grandparents are saving for his education. I shudder to think what his poor mother would do if he joined the police department instead. She's a single parent; Doug is all she has." Sammie had to stop to take a breath. "You're going to have to do something, Jake. Before it gets out of hand."

"There's no shame in being a cop, Sammie."

"You know perfectly well how I feel about the subject."

They were quiet for a moment. Jake knew there was no sense arguing with her, this was one battle he wouldn't win. "Okay, I'll say something to him next time I see him. I'll mention the paperwork and the long hours. I'll try to make it sound as dull as possible."

"Thank you."

"Now, if you're finished busting my butt—"

"What's playing at the theater?" She had never seen anyone love going to the movies as much as Jake, and she suspected it was his way of escaping.

"That new Clint Eastwood movie I was telling you about."

"Forget it."

"Why?" There was surprise in his voice.

"Because it's my turn to choose. You promised last time when I sat through two hours of Arnold Schwarzenegger."

"What do you want to see?"

"That one with Meryl Streep. She loses a son to bone cancer and falls in love with his doctor."

"Oh, for Pete's sake!" he muttered in disgust.

"We had a deal, Flannery. I can always ask Ruby to go with me, you know," she added, letting him know under no circumstances was she bound to him if he refused to keep up his end of the bargain. Besides, Jake hated going to the movies alone. "A deal's a deal," she reminded.

She loved Meryl Streep and if the truth were known, she didn't like going to the movies alone either.

"Have you always been this bossy or did it start with the pregnancy?" he said at last.

"So what's it going to be, Flannery?"

"What's the name of the movie?"

"*Too Many Tears.*"

"Oh, Jeez!" He was quiet for a moment. "I'll pick you up in half an hour."

When Jake arrived, Sammie had already changed into a pair of maternity jeans. "Come into the bedroom," she said, taking his hand. "I want to show you the new crib." She led him into the room and motioned to the light oak baby bed. "It took me two nights to put it together," she confessed. "I kept messing up."

Jake looked at her, a perplexed frown on his face. "Why didn't you call me, Sammie? I would have put it together for you."

She shrugged. "I figured—"

"You figured you'd rather do it yourself than have to ask for help," he interrupted. "Am I right?"

"You have enough going on in your life, Jake. I don't want to keep bugging you."

He stepped closer and put his arms on her shoulders. "We had an agreement. You'd call me for anything."

She glanced away, shaken by the piercing

black eyes that seemed to look right through her. "I don't want you feeling sorry for me, Jake."

He sighed and pulled her into his arms. There were times, such as this, when he wondered why such a strong independent woman had married in the first place. Of course, Nathan wouldn't have threatened that independence, he would have welcomed it. Caught up in his own world, a bit self-centered at times, Nathan Webster would never have tolerated a woman with too many needs of her own.

Jake liked to be needed once in a while.

"I don't feel sorry for you, Sammie," he said. "But I told you from the beginning that I would be here for you."

His chest was big and warm. With her ear pressed against it, Sammie felt his voice reverberate. It was comforting. She raised her head. "How long are you going to carry on this guilt trip, Jake? You weren't responsible for Nathan's death any more than I was."

He stiffened. All the warmth left his eyes. "I don't know what you're talking about."

"You still feel guilty because you couldn't prevent it. I don't hold you responsible for the shooting, Jake. Nathan *chose* to be a cop. He knew the risks."

"We're going to be late for the movie."

"Right." She was irritated. In a huff, she turned toward the door. "Anytime I try to square things between us, you pull away."

He reached out, closed his hand around her wrist. "Stop."

She faced him. "What?"

He hesitated. "I don't feel comfortable talking about Nathan's death. I never have. I listened to you talk about it in the beginning because I thought it was necessary for you. But it's still hard for me."

"Sometimes I feel like I've dealt with Nathan's death better than you," she said honestly. "Maybe you should talk to someone about your feelings. A professional."

"You're suggesting I see a shrink?" He gave a grunt. "How would that look? Here I am, protecting the good citizens of Atlanta, and I'm seeing someone for emotional problems. No, Sammie, I have to deal with this in my own way."

"Don't let it destroy your life, Jake," she said, remembering he'd offered her pretty much the same advice in the beginning. Why had he chosen to ignore it?

Jake was still thinking of their conversation as he sat in the dark theater and wondered what moron had written the plot line for the movie they were watching. The main characters were thrust into one depressing situation after the other, and Jake couldn't wait for somebody to die so they'd wrap it up and he could go home. It wasn't until he'd heard Sammie sniff several times that he realized she was crying.

He leaned close, caught a whiff of something nice. Sammie always smelled like freshly picked flowers. "Are you okay?" he asked.

She reached for his hand and held it tightly. Finally, she nodded.

Her hand felt small and frail in his. He studied her sorrowful expression. He was certain all this emotional upheaval couldn't be good for her or the baby. "We don't have to stay," he whispered. "Would you like to leave?"

She looked at him as though he'd lost his mind. Her eyes glistened with tears. "Are you crazy? This is the best movie I've seen in months."

Jake shook his head, slid down farther in his seat, and closed his eyes. Women! Who could figure them? Maybe he could sleep through the rest of this sorry picture. He had a mean thought. Maybe he should suggest that hardened criminals be forced to watch the film for punishment. Who knows, they might do away with capital punishment after all.

Sammie was still tearful when they left the theater. "Are you sure you're okay?" Jake asked around a wide yawn as he helped her into his Jeep. He worried about her. She tried to act so independent but he suspected, deep down, she wasn't as brave as she pretended.

"I'm okay," she said, then sighed wistfully. "Now that I know Carol and John will be happy. I know it will be tough for Carol at first, losing her son and all, but with John's love she'll make it. Did you see the way they looked at each other?"

Jake was still leaning in the door studying her cautiously. "You know it was just a movie, right?" She gave him a funny look as he closed the door and walked around to the other side.

"Didn't you enjoy it?" she asked when he joined her in the front seat. "Didn't it speak to you somehow?"

He stabbed his key into the ignition and cranked the engine. "Yeah, it spoke to me, all right. It told me next time I let you decide on the movie, I should turn my gun on myself and pull the trigger." He regretted the words the minute they left his mouth. He glanced at her quickly. "Gee, I'm sorry, Sammie. I didn't—"

"It's okay. I know you didn't mean anything by it."

"I don't always think before I talk."

"It's *okay*," she insisted.

He pulled out of the parking lot. "Tell you what. How about we stop and get an ice cream on the way home."

She brightened instantly. "Hot fudge sundae?"

"If that's what you want."

Sammie was licking her lips by the time they arrived at the ice-cream parlor. She stood behind Jake in the line. "Tell them to put extra hot fudge on it," she whispered. He nodded. "And nuts. I like nuts. And see if they'll give you two cherries instead of one. You're ordering me a large one, right?"

He looked at her. "Would you like to order it?"

She shook her head. "I don't want them to know it's for me."

Jake turned his attention to the front as one of the servers asked him what he wanted. "Give me one of those extra large sundaes," he said. "The one that serves three." He felt Sammie nudge him hard in the back. "And I want extra toppings." He turned to Sammie. "Hon, you did say you wanted extra toppings on your sundae, didn't you?" he called out loudly, drawing attention from everybody in the place. Her face flamed. He turned back to the counter. "Yeah, give her extra everything. As for me, I'd like a small diet drink. I'm watching my waistline."

"I hate you, Jake Flannery," Sammie hissed as he made her carry her dessert across the restaurant. He chose a table clear on the other side so she had to walk in front of the other customers. They took a seat. "You know I can't possibly eat all this."

"Yeah, but I have all the faith in the world you'll give it your best shot."

"You're trying to get back at me for making you sit through that movie."

He grinned. "Now that you mention it . . ."

She ate for a moment in silence. "You're welcome to have some." When he shook his head, she changed the subject. "So, when are you and what's-her-name going out? The dispatcher," she added when he shot her a blank look.

"Her name is Helen. We're going out next week."

"You don't waste any time. Where are you taking her?"

"To bed," he said, knowing that would get her riled.

"That's sick. You don't even know her."

"Okay, I'll take her to dinner first. Then we'll hit the sack."

She knew he was teasing her. She supposed she deserved it for asking about his personal life. Sometimes he didn't mind discussing it, sometimes he did. "Why don't you take her to that Italian restaurant you took me to last month? What's the name of it?" She snapped her fingers, trying to think.

"The Crusty Loaf?"

"Yes, that's the one. Where they serve hot bread beforehand."

He shrugged. "Maybe I will."

She gave him a funny look.

"What?"

"Nothing."

"Tell me."

"It's just, I feel funny telling you where to take another woman, you know? I know it's silly—"

He reached across the table and squeezed her hand. "It's not silly."

She shrugged. It bothered her to think of him shaving and showering and dressing up for a date. Not that Jake ever really dressed up. She didn't want to think of him gazing across a candle-lit table at another woman, kissing her good night at her door or taking her inside and—No, she wouldn't think about him making love to someone. "Maybe I'm a little jealous," she said at last.

That surprised him. "Why?"

She hesitated. "Because you've spent so much time with me the past six months. I mean, I know we're not romantically involved, but you've always been there for me."

He continued to hold her hand. "I'll always be here for you, Sammie. That's not going to change no matter what." She knew he meant well. But she also knew that if he became seriously involved with another woman, she would have to let go, get out of the picture altogether. It was selfish of her to worry about herself, she knew. Especially when Jake had done so much. She needed to prepare herself for the day he stopped coming around.

Jake wondered about the pensive look on her face. What was she thinking? They'd grown so close these past six months that he sometimes felt he could read her mind. This time he didn't have a clue. "I'd better take you home," he said.

"It's late, and you've probably got two dozen dogs to clip tomorrow." As he helped her out of the booth, he asked, "How much longer do you plan to work?"

"As long as I can. I'd rather take the time off with the baby. I've got someone coming in to do the grooming while I'm gone."

He led her out the door and to his Jeep. "Just don't overdo it," he said. "I don't want anything happening to you." He kissed her on her forehead and helped her inside.

THREE

It was ridiculous to feel the way she did. Sammie tried to concentrate on the *Unsolved Mysteries* program before her, but she couldn't keep her mind off Jake. What was he doing? Had he and Helen arrived at the restaurant yet? What was he wearing? Probably jeans and a cotton shirt and that navy blazer she liked so well.

"It's none of your business," she told herself and focused on the show where a woman claimed she'd been reincarnated from someone who'd lived during the Revolutionary War. But it was useless. Sammie decided to grab one of her newer magazines and take a warm bubble bath instead. She was jumpy tonight. Could it have anything to do with the baby? She placed her open palms against her stomach. The baby had moved several times today. In the beginning she'd noticed a strange fluttering inside, soft as a butterfly's wings, and she had called everybody she knew to tell them the baby had moved for the first time. Jake had pretended to be excited for her, but she knew he probably thought it was no big deal.

Jake. She had no right to think about him or wonder about his relationships with other women. Especially in her condition. Not that Jake ever made her feel unattractive or clumsy. He made her feel . . . she paused. Cherished and protected. Something she'd never felt before, not even with Nathan, whose short temper and low frustration level had made it impossible for her to share her worries or disappointments with him.

Jake. Big and gruff and always in control. He would make any woman feel safe. But he had never indicated he was interested in anything more than friendship. He had every right to see other women. Heaven knows he'd done enough for her. She only wished he hadn't done it all out of guilt.

It was almost midnight when Sammie heard someone tap on her door. She hadn't been able to fall asleep so she'd picked up a book instead. Now, she climbed out of bed, hurried into the next room and peered through the peephole. Jake was standing on the other side. She unlocked the door and opened it.

"You checked the peephole first, right?"

"Of course I did. What are you doing here?"

He looked concerned. "I saw your lights on when I drove by. Is something wrong?"

"Everything's fine, Jake. I was just reading. You want a cold beer?"

He looked glad she had invited him. "A soft drink would be nice. I'll only stay five minutes." He walked through the door and closed it behind him, then followed Sammie into the kitchen where she was in the process of pulling a diet drink out of the refrigerator.

"Where's Helen?" she asked as she handed him the can.

"I just dropped her off."

Sammie felt self-conscious in her maternity gown. She sat down at the table and tucked one leg beneath her. "So how'd it go?"

He shrugged as he popped open his drink. "Okay, I guess."

"Just *okay*?"

He joined her at the table. "What do you want me to say? We had dinner, then I took her home."

"What's her place like?"

"I don't know, I didn't go inside."

She felt silly for the relief that washed over her. "So, are you going to see her again?"

He paused, his soda can halfway to his lips. "What is this, an interrogation?"

She blushed. "You've never minded telling me about your dates before."

He shifted in his chair. He looked uncomfortable. "Maybe I don't want to anymore."

"Why?"

He didn't know *why* he was feeling like he was. "I don't know. Maybe—" He grinned, reached out and tweaked her nose. "Maybe I don't think it's any of your business, fatso."

"Call me fat again and I'll handcuff you to the fire hydrant downstairs where the dogs go to the bathroom." Still, she couldn't very well argue with the fact that it was none of her business. "Okay, I'll stop being nosy. Are we still getting together tomorrow night?"

"Unless I have to work late. Why don't I call you from the office tomorrow afternoon?" He finished his drink and carried the can to the trash. "I've got to go. Come walk me to the door so you can lock up."

He put his hand at the small of her back while she walked with him, and it felt big and warm against her. He seemed taller standing next to her in her bare feet, his shoulders wider in the jacket. He wore the after-shave she'd given him for his birthday the month before.

At the door, Jake turned and faced her. She smelled of soap and body lotion. Her gown was delicate, printed in soft pastel flowers. He was glad some women still wore gowns instead of those baggy shirts. Her thick hair, normally styled in a perfect shoulder-length pageboy, was slightly mussed. "Now, go in there and turn off the light and get some sleep," he said. "I'm going to be watching from the parking lot below." He kissed her on the forehead, then waited outside the door until he heard all three locks click into place.

Sammie and Ruby were just sitting down to lunch when Jake called the next day. "Do you have a nice maternity dress?" he asked when Sammie answered.

"Yes, why?"

"Wear it. I'll pick you up at six-thirty tonight."

"Are you always this bossy?"

"If I weren't, you'd walk all over me."

"Okay, so where are we going?"

"You'll see. Got to go." He hung up the phone before she could question him further.

Sammie wondered the rest of the afternoon where Jake was taking her and couldn't wait to get home to shower and dress. "Look at you," she said to her reflection. "You'd think you were Barbie going to the dance with Ken. Grow up, Samantha."

She did a double take when she opened her door and found Jake on the other side wearing charcoal slacks, a dress shirt, and a beige jacket. "My, don't you look nice," she said. "You're even wearing real shoes."

"You look nice too." His eyes dropped to the

dark blue linen dress appreciatively, where only the slightest paunch was noticeable. They spent so much time together that people often mistook him for the father-to-be, but it didn't bother him in the least. Sammie was the one who got all red-faced over it. "You ready to go?" he said, offering his arm.

"Are we riding in one of those pumpkin carriages tonight?"

He shook his head. "Naw, all I could come up with was a four-by-four."

Jake drove toward the city, telling her about his day. Someone he'd convicted almost ten years before had gotten out on parole a month ago. He'd heard the guy was already selling on the street. "I'm going to catch him," he said, with conviction. "Maybe not today or the next day, but sooner or later I'll get him. And if he's dealing, I'm going to see that he goes back for a long, long time."

"Is he dangerous?" Sammie asked.

"Define dangerous."

"Does he carry a weapon?"

"Most of them do. We got ten-year-olds carrying guns today."

She sighed heavily. "Jake, how are you ever going to have a life?"

The question made absolutely no sense to him. He glanced at her. "What do you mean?"

"How are you ever going to have a family when your job is so dangerous?"

He looked surprised. "Who said I wanted a family? If I remember correctly, I told you I didn't."

"So you're prepared to spend the rest of your life living solely for your job?"

"I'm not living for my job. I do other things."

"Like what?"

He thought about it. "I bowl. I play softball."

"For the police department."

"I go out."

"With men and women who work for the police department. Face it, Flannery, you eat, sleep, and breathe the police department."

He stopped at a red light and looked at her. "So what's wrong with that? I've been with the department for fifteen years, that's who I am."

"You're not afraid of dying?"

"So that's what this is all about." The light changed and he drove on, a thoughtful expression on his face. "Let me put it to you this way, Sammie. I'd much rather be shot down doing something I believe in and enjoy than living to a ripe old age doing something I hate just to feel safe."

She pondered that. There was wisdom in what he said, she supposed, but it didn't stop her from worrying about him.

The Peachtree Inn was located in the heart of Atlanta's historic district, a massive antebellum home famous for its veal and chicken dishes.

As Jake pulled up at the door, two uniformed men hurried to assist them. One helped her out, the other took Jake's keys and moved the car to the back of the building so the next customer could pull up.

"Fancy place," Sammie said as Jake escorted her through the front door and down a long hall where a hostess waited. "What's the occasion?"

"This is just my way of thanking you for all those great meals on Thursday nights."

"You don't have to thank me, I enjoy doing it."

They were led to a table where a waiter appeared out of nowhere to take a drink order. Jake ordered a mixed drink, Sammie ordered orange juice. When the drinks arrived, he toasted her. "To the prettiest girl in the room."

"You're too kind," she said, taking a sip of her juice. "I know what I am."

He frowned and set his glass down. "And what are you?"

"I'm almost eight months pregnant. I'm retaining fluid, I waddle like a duck when I walk, I'm moody. Not a pretty sight."

"I think you're beautiful."

She was touched. Nevertheless, she grinned. "Are you flirting with me, Jake?" she asked. "Because if you are, I think I should warn you, nothing is going to happen between us at the end of the night."

He pretended to look disappointed. "You

mean I'm not going to score?" He shrugged. "Oh well, I've been turned down before."

"I doubt that. Nathan once told me you had quite a reputation with the ladies. That's one of the reasons I didn't want him spending so much time with you."

"That was a long time ago. I've calmed down since then. I'm getting too old for that sort of thing."

She was quiet for a minute. "I sometimes wonder if I'll ever date again."

He was plainly shocked by the comment. "I hardly think this is the time to be thinking about your love life, Sammie."

She was amused by the disturbed look on his face. "Not now, silly. Later." When he continued to stare at her as though he thought her daft, she went on. "You don't expect me to sit in the house and mourn forever, do you? I'm thirty years old, Jake. I still have time to start over."

He didn't say anything right away. "I guess I never thought about it, you meeting someone else, maybe remarrying." He was pensive for a moment. "You're not going to do anything in the near future?"

She laughed and patted her belly. "Obviously."

"And you'll introduce me to this person when the time comes? I have to approve of him, you know. I won't allow my niece or nephew to be raised by some maniac."

"Give me a little credit," she said indignantly. When he didn't look satisfied, she reached across the table and patted his hand. "We've got plenty of time to fight about it, Jake, but when the time comes, I promise you'll have a say."

Jake was prevented from answering when the waiter appeared to take their order. "Do you know what you want?" he asked Sammie.

She glanced at her menu. "I'll have the stuffed chicken breast over wild rice," she said.

"And I'll take the veal special," Jake told the man. He glanced up and found Sammie looking at him with shock and disbelief. He blinked. "What?"

"You're not going to eat a baby calf, are you?"

Jake looked from her to the waiter and back. Her eyes were large and luminous. He leaned closer. "Honey, this place specializes in veal dishes."

"That doesn't mean you have to eat it. Don't you know how they treat those poor creatures?" Looking near tears, she put her napkin down. "I couldn't possibly sit here and watch you eat a baby calf."

Jake squirmed in his chair and eyed the waiter who looked as though he'd rather be someplace else. "She's a little emotional tonight," he said, then opened his menu once more. "I think I'll have the New York strip instead." He glanced at Sammie. "It wouldn't bother you if I ate a *grown* cow, would it? One who'd already experienced life to the fullest?"

"Don't make fun of me, Jake. This is something I feel strongly about."

He closed his menu and handed it to the waiter. "Thanks."

Sammie waited until they were alone to speak. "Thank you, Jake."

"I'm only doing it 'cause you're pregnant and might cause a scene if I don't. I happen to like veal." He regarded her for a moment, then chuckled. "Damned if you aren't the bossiest woman I ever met. I'll bet you gave old Nathan a run for his money."

"I'm not bossy. A little outspoken at times, maybe."

"Yeah, like from dawn till dusk."

"Nathan liked it that I was independent."

He didn't doubt it for a minute. "Frankly, I liked it better the old way, when the man had the upper hand."

"Why am I not surprised?"

"Women didn't have it so bad. They knew they could count on the old man to bring home the bacon. All they had to do was sit home and look pretty." He was teasing her now because it was so much fun to get a rise out of her.

Sammie laughed in spite of herself. "Jake, I love you to death, but you are so far off base it's

Charlotte Hughes

52

pathetic. No wonder you have to date brain-dead women."

He looked insulted. "What do you mean? I date intelligent women."

"Then why they put up with your views and opinions is beyond me. I guess that's where your club comes in handy. You hit 'em over the head once or twice and they'll go along with anything you say."

"Why should I have to use my nightstick when I've got charm and good looks to woo them?"

"I fell right into that one, didn't I?"

He grinned. "So how do you think it's supposed to be between a man and woman, Miss Authority-on-Life-and-Love?"

"Fifty-fifty."

"You don't want a man opening doors for you or pulling out your chair?"

"I didn't say that at all."

"Aha! I got'cha."

"That's really not what it's all about." She paused. "If a man does those things for me, I'll probably do something in return like cook his favorite meal or bake him a cake. But I'm not going to do it because it's expected of me. I'm going to do it because I genuinely enjoy cooking."

He looked smug. "Who is going to mow the grass and keep the car in good running order?"

"The person who is better at it. The chores

don't have to be divided based on gender. A couple can swap around from time to time."

Jake leaned back in his chair, crossed his arms, then cocked his head to one side. "Okay, let's talk about sex."

Sammie shifted in her own seat but was determined not to let him know she was the least bit uncomfortable. "Okay, what about it?"

"Who's in charge?"

She blinked. "Why does anyone have to be in charge?"

" 'Cause that's the way I like it."

She met his gaze. "You're saying you don't like the woman taking the initiative?"

"I might let her some of the time."

"*Let* her?"

"But only if she knows what she's doing."

"I see."

"It's like this. I don't want to be bored on the job, and I don't want to be bored in the sack." He was clearly trying to get her riled now.

"There's nothing wrong with showing somebody what you like . . . what makes you feel good. But it works both ways, you know. The woman should be able to communicate the same to a man."

"Most women like what I do to them just fine."

The comment annoyed her. Sammie was thankful when the waiter returned with their salads. She didn't start on it right away. "Let me just say this, Jake. When you fall in love with someone, you don't really worry about all those things. When two people are in love, each one of them is concerned about making the other one happy or taking the load off. At least that's the way it should be."

He watched the emotions on her face as she talked, and couldn't help but wonder when she'd experienced that kind of love. "Is that the way it was for you and Nathan?" he asked, unable to resist probing.

She looked away. "It could have been." She turned back to him. "Nathan and I had our problems. I wasn't crazy about his being a cop. He thought marriage came with too many demands. And, of course, there was that temper of his. He could be a regular hothead bull in the china shop at times."

"Did he ever hurt you?"

She shook her head. "I think he knew better." She sighed and picked up her fork. "But enough of that, let's talk about something else. You know what Sunday is?"

Jake was still thinking about her and Nathan. He wondered if she knew he'd been sleeping around. Until now, she'd never discussed their marital problems with him. But he'd suspected. "No, what?" he said, deciding it was best to move to another subject.

"We start our prepared childbirth class."

When he looked surprised, she went on. "You're not going to back out on me, I hope."

He wasn't looking forward to it. But what could he do, he'd already promised. Nathan had let her down a number of times; he wasn't going to. "I'll be there."

FOUR

The narcotics unit was located on the second floor of the police department. Except for the captain's, there were no private offices, and so the work areas were partitioned to allow a certain amount of privacy. Jake was hardly ever in his cubicle. Most of his time was spent on the streets, checking with his contacts, looking for new faces and old, issuing search warrants and performing them. Although he was extremely careful with his men, it was a known fact that he sometimes broke the rules when he had to. Some on the street claimed he was as dangerous as those he arrested. Jake didn't care. He liked to keep the bad guys guessing.

The phone on his desk rang, and Jake grabbed it. "Flannery."

"This is Carl."

Carl was an informant. He'd been working

with Jake for six months in exchange for immunity on a drug bust. "You got something for me?" Jake asked.

"I hear you're looking for Bo Jenkins. The guy who just got out on parole."

"Have you seen him?"

"He and his brother opened a store over on Seventy-fifth. They sell milk, bread, soft drinks, and a little cocaine on the side."

"No kidding? They got any guns?"

"You might say that. I've seen them with a Colt Python .357 magnum and a .12-gauge shotgun."

"Thanks, Carl." Jake hung up the phone and called a meeting with himself and the other men on his team.

"I don't know if either of you remember Bo Jenkins," he said. "Tall, wiry-framed guy with acne scars?"

"I remember him," a heavyweight named Bob said. "He's mean as a rattlesnake."

"Not to mention elusive," Jake said. "But I just learned he and his brother are dealing out of a store on 75th Street. I'm getting a search warrant. You guys be ready to go."

The store was actually a house converted into a store. Once the police van pulled up out front, the four-man narcotics team wasted no time. When they found the front door locked, Bob rushed forward with a sixteen-pound sledge-hammer. He swung it once and the door exploded.

Jake, holding a Smith & Wesson Model 38, entered the store, yelling, "Police!"

The plump elderly black woman sitting behind the cash register ducked behind the counter as the detectives stormed the place. "Don't shoot!" she cried. "I got my grandbaby with me." She threw her body on a toddler who was sleeping on a blanket nearby. The little one awoke with a start and began screaming.

Jake hurried behind the counter while his men checked the place. "Get up," he told the woman, lowering his gun. "We aren't going to harm you or the child." He felt crummy for scaring the baby. "See if you can calm her down."

The woman clamored to her feet, picking up her crying granddaughter. "It's okay, sweetie," she said, hugging her tight.

Jake studied the woman. She was white-headed and big-bosomed, wearing a flowered dress. She finally got the baby to stop crying. "Where's Bo Jenkins?" he asked.

The woman gave him a blank look. "I don't know nobody by that name, Officer."

She was shaking so badly, he was certain she was telling the truth. "Who are you working for?"

"Somebody named Lamar somethin'-or-other."

Two of his men returned. "Nobody in the back," one said. "We're going to have a look outside while the others search inside."

The old woman was still trembling. Actually, she looked like she might have a stroke. "What's your name?" Jake asked her.

"Mary Black. I live down the street. Heard there was a job to be had here so I asked about it. I got my three grandchildren living with me. I need the money."

"When does your boss come around?"

"I don't see much of him. I open up in the morning and close the place each night. I pay for deliveries out of the cash register. He calls me once in a while to see how business is going. All I care about is him showing up on payday, which he always does."

"Why was the front door locked?"

"I was just locking up for the day, Officer."

Jake stuffed his gun in the back of his pants. "Well, we have a search warrant, Miss Black," he said, laying the form on the counter where she could see it. "You won't mind if we take a look around." He realized he was a bit late in telling her. He could hear his men taking the place apart.

"Just don't make no mess," she pleaded. "I need this job."

An hour later they exited the store with nothing. One of the men shook his head sadly. "Man,

I feel terrible. I think we scared that poor old lady and her granddaughter something fierce."

"I don't get it," Jake said, feeling foolish as they climbed into the van. "This informant usually knows what he's talking about. Something's not right."

Lakewood Hospital was a white three-story V-shaped building with a green-tiled roof, only fifteen minutes from Sammie's apartment. After Jake parked and helped her out of the car, she thanked him once again for agreeing to be her coach.

"You won't regret this," she told him.

He took the blanket and pillow they were supposed to bring to class. "Yeah, but you can't guarantee that, can you?"

Sammie laughed. She had been looking forward to the class all day. She had just entered her eighth month, and the baby was kicking. Finally, after all these months, it looked as though there was an end in sight. "No, I can't," she said at last.

"Just kidding," he said, taking her hand and squeezing it. He was nervous for reasons he couldn't explain.

They made their way inside the front entrance and to the information counter where they were told to go to the second floor. Inside the classroom area, ten other couples of various ages waited for the lesson to begin. The women were all in advanced stages of pregnancy. Sammie, who'd been feeling like everyone around her was getting smaller as she was getting bigger, felt right at home.

The instructor was a pert brunette who introduced herself as Sally Waters and informed them they were about to embark on one of the most meaningful experiences of their lives. "Before we get started, though, you're going to see a film of an actual childbirth."

Jake leaned close to Sammie. "You didn't tell me we were going to see a film," he whispered accusingly.

She shrugged. "How was I supposed to know?"

Sally continued. "Now, I must warn you, the film is very graphic. But it should give you some idea of what to expect." She turned off the lights and started the projector. The film began with the expectant couple arriving at the hospital, all smiles, very much looking forward to the big event. Next, the nurses settled the mother-to-be in the labor room and hooked up the monitor. Before long the woman had gone from early labor to active labor, and she was no longer smiling. Her husband had a weary is-this-ever-gonna-be-over? look on his face.

"Now, they're going into the delivery room," Sally announced.

Jake was not prepared for the rest of the film.

Although policemen sometimes delivered babies, he had not. He grimaced as he watched the baby struggle to get out. "The baby's not going to fit through," he whispered to Sammie.

"Now, we're going to see the episiotomy," announced Sally.

Jake shuddered as the doctor made it possible for the baby's head to fit through the opening. "I guess I was wrong," he said weakly.

Finally, the baby was delivered, a tiny slippery bundle covered with a white substance Sally called vernix. Once again, the couple was smiling, and Jake thought the new mother looked like she was ready for a vacation.

The film ended, and Sally reached up to turn on the lights. "What did you think?" she asked.

Jake looked at Sammie. "I'll tell you what I think," he whispered. "I think you've got the wrong guy."

"Shhh!" Sammie nudged him hard and listened as Sally answered questions about the film.

"Next meeting I'm going to take you on a tour of our labor and delivery area," the instructor said, "but now, I want to spend the next few minutes discussing prepared childbirth and why we believe the techniques offered will help you have a safe, more meaningful delivery. We'll also touch on nutrition and exercise. After that we'll learn some relaxation techniques that you can practice at home this week."

By the time they were instructed to move to

the floor with their blankets and pillows, Jake was feeling overwhelmed by all he'd learned.

Sally waited until everyone was comfortably situated around the room. "Okay, you'll have to share your pillow with your partner, but I want you to lie side by side. We're going to listen to music." She walked over to a cassette player and switched it on, then dimmed the lights.

"I feel stupid," Jake said, lying beside Sammie on the pillow. "I'm glad nobody at headquarters is here to witness this."

"Don't worry," she said out of the side of her mouth. "Nobody has to know you might have an ounce of sensitivity in you."

The music began, a classical piece, and they were instructed to lie there quietly.

"*Feel* the music," Sally said in a soothing voice. "Let it enter your body. Close your eyes and try to imagine a scene in which you're totally at ease."

"Is this some kind of New Age thing?" Jake whispered.

Sammie ignored him, giving in to the feeling of peacefulness that was drifting over her. After a while, she was so relaxed, she half feared falling asleep. She was only vaguely aware when Sally spoke again.

"Gentlemen, I now want you to sit up beside your wife." She waited until the men did so. "While the music is playing softly, I want you to reach up and stroke your wife's forehead. Lightly and gently. That's right."

Jake reached up and placed a hand on Sammie's forehead, then caressed it. Her eyes fluttered open, met his briefly, then closed once more.

"Ladies, take a deep breath and hold it for several seconds, then exhale. Do it again. And as you're doing so, pretend you're blowing away all the worries and frustrations of the day. Husbands, stroke your wife's arms now. Yes, that's right. Move to her abdomen. Stroke and caress."

Jake paused, obviously not sure what to do. Sammie opened her eyes. "It's okay," she said.

He moved his hand over the mound, feeling very self-conscious. He tossed her a look of surprise. "It's firm. I thought it would feel—" He paused.

"Like a giant marshmallow?" she grinned.

"Something like that." He continued touching her, feeling more comfortable. He was fascinated, then, much to his surprise, aroused. She had never looked sexier to him. He snatched his hand away, saw Sammie's look of surprise, but decided to ignore it. Thankfully, Sally chose that moment to end the class. The couples stood and folded their blankets, chatting with their neighbors while Sally reminded them of the next class.

"How'd I do?" Jake asked a few minutes later as he helped Sammie into his Jeep.

"You did fine," she said, feeling slightly disoriented and maybe a little emotional after all they'd shared. She waited for him to join her in the front seat. "You need to loosen up a bit, though. You act like I'm going to break."

He stared straight ahead. "It just doesn't seem right."

"What? You touching me?" Sammie waited for him to deny it. When he didn't, she felt hurt. He was obviously repulsed by her swollen body. Why else would he snatch his hand away? She looked out her window. "I'll tell you what's not right," she replied angrily. "It's not right that I have to go through this pregnancy without my husband beside me. It's not right that I'm going to have to bring a baby into the world without a father. That's what's not right!" She was almost shouting. She didn't realize she was crying until a tear slid silently down her cheek. Jake was staring at her as though he'd accidentally grabbed the wrong pregnant woman when he left. "And here you are bitching because you had to go to one sorry class with me. Well, you can just forget it." She opened the door.

"What the hell are you doing?" he said in disbelief.

"I'm walking home."

"No, hell no, you're not. Close the door!"

She climbed out of the Jeep and slammed the door so hard, the car shook.

Jake muttered a string of curse words, climbed out and hurried around to her side. She was already walking off in the opposite direction. "Would you wait just a damn minute?" he said, closing his hand around her wrist and bringing her to a halt. He turned her around, placing his hands on her shoulders. "I don't know what I said to get you so fired up, but whatever it was, I certainly didn't mean it the way you took it."

The tears were streaming down her cheeks. "You said it didn't feel right touching me," she managed.

"I only meant it should be Nathan touching you, not me."

"Nathan's dead, Jake. He *can't* touch me. No matter how *desperately* I need him to. I accepted that fact months ago. Why can't you?"

He felt stupid standing in the middle of the parking lot arguing with her. "It's hard sometimes," he confessed, fixing her with a sincere gaze.

She jerked away from him. "You want to know what's hard? It's hard climbing into an empty bed each night in those damn flannel maternity gowns that are supposed to keep you so warm, you won't think about being held. It's hard feeling the baby kick and not being able to share it with someone. But most of all—" She paused as fresh tears filled her eyes. "It's hard going through life not being touched by someone, *anyone*."

He felt as though someone had put a knife through his heart and twisted it. "Oh, Sammie."

He pulled her into his arms. This time she didn't resist.

"You think I'm terrible, don't you?" she managed through a sob. "To want to be held and touched when my husband hasn't even been dead a year."

Jake swallowed, and it was obvious he was feeling emotional as well. "I don't think you're terrible, babe. I think you're perfectly normal to want those things. I'm just sorry I didn't see it. I thought everything was fine, but I keep forgetting how important it is for you to appear tough and independent." He pulled away and looked into her eyes. "Why didn't you tell me what you were feeling?" When she merely shrugged, he went on. "Is it so hard for you to tell someone you need something?"

"You're one to talk, Jake Flannery."

"Yeah, but us guys *are* tougher and need less." He grinned at the look she gave him. "Just kidding," he said, drawing her against him once more, or as close as he could in her condition. "I promise I'll start touching you," he said. "I'll give you back rubs in front of the TV."

"It doesn't—" She paused. "—repulse you?"

He frowned. "What, that you're pregnant?" He shook his head emphatically. "I think you're downright adorable. And sexy, too, despite what you say."

She looked doubtful. "Don't overdo it, Jake."

"I swear it's the truth." He pulled back, put a

finger under her chin and tilted her face back so that she was looking at him. "Have I ever said or done anything to make you feel unattractive?"

"No." She leaned against his broad chest as he simply held her. "This feels so nice," she confessed. "You won't tell anyone I went to pieces in the parking lot?"

He shook his head again. "Nobody'll ever have to know you had a weak moment."

"I suppose you'll expect me to buy you an ice-cream cone in return."

He didn't particularly like ice cream, but it was enough that she did. "Yep," he said. "That should be payment enough." He walked her back to the Jeep with his arm around her.

When Jake arrived at his place more than an hour later after seeing Sammie home, the phone was ringing. He picked it up on the third ring.

"Hello, stranger," a feminine voice said from the other end. "I was just about to give up on you."

"Hello, Helen." Jake tried to sound pleased to hear from the woman as he sank onto the sofa and reached for the remote control. "What's up?"

"I was just wondering why you didn't call tonight," she said, her tone hurt.

Jake hated it when women did that sort of

thing to him. "I was out. Doing a favor for a friend."

"Oh? Who's the friend?"

He decided since she was being so nosy he would tell her about Sammie. "Her husband was in my unit. He got killed seven months ago in the line of duty. She's pregnant and has nobody to go through it with her."

There was a moment's pause. "I see. And you, being the gentleman you are, have decided to help her."

He thought she might be making fun of him, and he was suddenly in a hurry to get off the phone. "Something like that, yeah." He forced a wide yawn. "Listen, if you don't mind, I'm really whipped. Why don't we talk tomorrow?"

"Sure." She sounded disappointed but was graceful about the brush-off.

Jake hung up the phone, thankful to be rid of her although he didn't understand why. Helen was attractive and amusing. He knew the guys in narcotics and homicide had placed bets on when he would climb into the sack with her. There was a time when Jake would have joined in the fun, but these days he had too much on his mind.

He gazed at the telephone for a moment, then snatched it up and dialed. Sammie answered on the other end. "I hope you weren't asleep."

"No, I just climbed into my ugly maternity gown," she said, then gave a brief laugh. "This is why I don't need a dog. If a man breaks into my place, he'll take one look at me and run the other way."

Jake chuckled. "I doubt it's as bad as all that."

"Trust me on this one, Jake."

"I've seen you in your maternity gown, Sammie. You look—" He tried to think of the right word.

"Like a hot-air balloon?"

"You look cuddly," he said, testing the word. It wasn't one he used often to describe a woman. "Like something a man would like to snuggle up to on a cold night. Maybe in front of a roaring fire."

"Hmmm. That sounds pretty good, Flannery. Did you get that out of a book?"

"Naw, it just sort of came to me. Listen, what are you doing for lunch tomorrow?"

"Probably eating a sub at the front counter with Ruby."

"Why don't I pick you up at noon?"

"Why?"

"So I can take you to lunch."

"Why?"

"What do you mean, why?"

She took a deep breath. "You're doing this because you feel sorry for me, aren't you? Because I broke down tonight and spilled my guts all over the hospital parking lot?"

"That's not why I'm doing it," he said impatiently. "I'm doing it because I enjoy your company. Why does everything have to be a battle between us?"

"What about Helen?"

"What about her?"

"Won't she be hurt that you didn't ask her? I mean, I'm not worried about her being jealous of me or anything. Lord, she only has to take one look at me to see that I'm no competition. But shouldn't you ask her?"

Jake sighed heavily into the telephone. He was almost sorry he'd called. "Look, I might as well tell you. I'm not interested in Helen. She's a nice lady and all, but I don't think there could ever be anything between us. Now, if you don't want to go to lunch tell me now so I can hang up and watch a little TV."

"Well, you don't have to get huffy about it, Jake," she said. "You called me, I didn't call you. Besides, I was only trying to figure out your motivation for inviting me. Now that I know I won't be interfering with your relationship with Helen, I'll be happy to go to lunch with you."

"You're not going to act like this *after* the baby comes, are you?"

"I pretty much act this way all the time. You should know, you've been around me the past seven months."

"Wishful thinking," he said. "I'll see you tomorrow."

FIVE

Captain John Mitchell was anxiously waiting for Jake early the next morning. The captain was a balding man with a bulldog face who never strayed far from his bottle of liquid antacid. He reached for it the second Jake walked through the door. It was no secret the two didn't get along. He tolerated Jake because he was one of the best detectives on the force. Jake dealt with the man the only way he knew how. He let whatever the captain said go in one ear and out the other.

"They ran a check on Mary Black," the captain said, then read from a list. "Alias Mary White, alias Mary-Alice Brown, alias Mary-Jane Green."

Jake looked as surprised as he felt. "Damn, she really gets around. And she looked so . . . so grandmotherly."

"Served time for forgery, breaking and entering, possession of heroin, illegal possession of firearms."

"So it was all just a big front," Jake said. "Including the baby." He gritted his teeth. "That's the part that pisses me off."

The captain nodded. "I thought we might—"

"I'm going back in," Jake said. "And this time the old bag gets hauled in with the rest of them."

"Get someone lined up to take the children," Mitchell said.

Jake nodded. "That's the hard part."

Sammie was waiting out front wearing light gray leggings and a baggy white blouse with embroidery accents when Jake pulled up in front of her shop shortly after twelve. "Sorry I'm late," he said as she climbed into his Jeep. "I got tied up."

"Literally?"

"Huh?" He blinked. "No, I was busy on a case."

"Well, one never knows in your line of work."

"It's not as dangerous as all that," he told her as he backed out of the parking spot. "Most of the time it's rather boring."

"Don't feed me that, Jake. I know better."

He decided it best just to drop the subject.

He pulled into a parking space near a sandwich and pizza shop ten minutes later. Inside it was cool and smelled of yeast. They had just been seated and given their drinks when Sammie grabbed her stomach and held it for a moment. Jake almost knocked over his iced tea. "What is it?" he demanded. "Is this *it*?" He wondered how he'd ever help her after attending only one childbirth class. He wondered how he'd ever get her to the hospital in the afternoon lunch traffic.

She shook her head. "No, these are just Braxton-Hicks contractions. I've been having them a lot the past few days."

"Who the hell is Braxton Hicks?"

"I don't know. That's just what they call them."

"What should we do?"

She picked up her menu. "They'll pass. Do you want to order bread sticks for an appetizer?"

"I don't care." He leaned closer. "How do you *know* they'll pass?"

"Because it's not time for the baby, silly." The waitress appeared and Sammie turned to her. "We're going to have the bread sticks with cheese for an appetizer," she said. "And for my lunch, I'd like a salad with extra blue-cheese dressing, and a steak-and-cheese grinder."

The waitress turned to Jake. "I'll just have a meatball sandwich," he said, not even bothering to look at his menu. He was still watching Sammie closely. Her cheeks were flushed but that was probably due to the heat. "Maybe you should call your doctor," he said, once the waitress had walked away. "I mean, how do you know you aren't going into early labor?"

"We'll know when actual labor begins, Jake. In the meantime, I'll just have to put up with these contractions. They're very mild, though sometimes they wake me up during the night. Do you think the waitress will bring the bread sticks before my salad?"

Jake stared back at her in disbelief. How she could think about bread sticks when he was afraid she'd give birth in a booth was beyond him. "I'll ask," he said, signaling the waitress while keeping his eyes fixed on Sammie.

Their meal came, and Jake watched Sammie devour the bread sticks, the salad, the grinder, and his bag of chips. She looked embarrassed. "I overslept this morning and missed breakfast."

"You want something else?" he asked politely. "A pizza, maybe?"

She laughed. "No, this will hold me until dinner. I only hope I don't continue to eat like this *after* the baby comes. I'll have to get a part-time job to be able to afford my groceries." She paused. "Jake, do I bore you?" she asked, changing the subject suddenly. When he looked surprised, she went on. "I mean, all I talk about these days is my pregnancy and the baby. Do you wish I'd talk about something else for a change?"

"Do I look bored?"

"I don't know. I can never tell what you're thinking. Still, I should probably talk about other things. Like, what you're doing at work these days? What *are* you doing at work these days?"

He wondered if she really wanted to know or if she was merely trying to be nice. "Well, right now I'm waiting on a judge to sign a search warrant so I can get inside someone's store and look for drugs and guns. If I can't do it this afternoon, I'll probably go first thing in the morning. Then, tomorrow afternoon I have to testify in court against a pimp who beat a hooker with a clothes hanger and—"

"Never mind, I don't think I want to know," she said quickly.

His eyes met hers. "Don't you want to know about the guy who's selling cans of glue to young teenagers at the bus station?"

"No."

"I didn't think so." He studied her expression. It was one of distaste. "You're never going to accept what I do so why pretend?"

"I suppose you think I should forget what happened to Nathan," she said.

"No, but I'm asking you to trust me to know how to take care of myself. I'm not as impatient and quick to act as—" He caught himself.

"As Nathan was," she said for him.

"I take my time, get a feel for the situation."

"You think I haven't told myself that, Jake?

But I'm still afraid. I've already lost a loved one. I don't want to lose another."

It surprised him that she would compare the love she had for Nathan to what she felt for him, but Jake knew she didn't mean it that way. He took her hand and squeezed it. "Listen to me, Sammie. I might break a lot of rules in the department, but I don't take unnecessary chances. Not on my life, not on the lives of my men. With Nathan—" He paused and shook his head. "Hell, I didn't know where he was half the time. I'd send him in one direction, he'd go in another. I complained, I even punched him in the jaw once when he did something totally stupid.

"The day Nathan was shot, we knew there'd be guns. We had a guy holding a shield. Nathan was supposed to be behind it." He paused again and sighed heavily.

"Nathan was a show-off," Sammie said, suspecting that's what Jake had wanted to say but didn't for fear of hurting her. "I think it was because there were so many cops in his family, and his father was sort of a hero. He took a bullet for another cop. Almost died." She paused. "And now, Nathan's a hero. At least as far as his family is concerned."

They were silent for a moment, each of them caught up in their own thoughts. "I'd better get you back," Jake said. "I'm sure you've got a dozen dogs who need haircuts."

He paid the check, even though she tried to

snatch it from him. "You paid for dinner last night," she said.

"And I'm paying for lunch today," he replied evenly. "You got a problem with that?"

"It's some kind of macho thing, isn't it? You can't stand the thought of a woman buying your lunch." She was getting him back for all the teasing he'd done to her earlier. "Now you'll expect sex in return."

He turned and patted her on the belly. "Believe me, it's the last thing on my mind right now." Liar, he thought. Pregnant or not, she was attractive as hell. Her body was lush and ripe and more sensual than a woman in her condition had any right to be. Sometimes, just before he went to sleep at night, he yearned to see what lay beneath her maternity dresses and he felt himself become aroused at the thought.

They left the restaurant a few minutes later, still carrying on their playful banter. Jake, cupping her elbow in his palm, assisted her down a short flight of stairs leading to the parking lot, taking care to see that she didn't stumble. He suddenly felt guilty for what he'd been thinking only two minutes earlier. He really was a jerk, he supposed. What kind of man thought about having sex with a woman one minute and protecting her the next?

When Sammie opened her door Thursday night, she was surprised to find Jake standing on the other side. "I didn't know you were coming to dinner tonight," she said. "You always call the night before to let me know if you can make it. I figured something came up."

"I'm sorry," he said, as she opened the door wide to let him through. "It's been a rough week. I've put in a lot of overtime. By the time I got home at the end of the day, I just fell into bed."

"Did something happen?"

He walked into the living room and slumped into a chair. "Yeah, that case we were working on. The grandmother was carrying several ounces of coke on her. She spilled her guts in exchange for immunity. We raided three other houses. Got who we were looking for."

"Anybody get hurt?"

"Just the bad guys. They tried to resist. We put a couple of them in the hospital."

"Well, thank God *you're* not hurt," she said, her gaze combing him for any injury no matter how small.

"I'm okay, Sammie," he insisted, then noticed how messy she looked. "What have you been doing?"

"Wallpapering."

He jumped from the chair. "What? Have you lost your mind?"

"No lectures tonight, please. Come look."

Shaking his head, Jake followed her inside the room which was to be the nursery. One of the walls was completely papered, and she had started on the second one. "How the hell did you climb that ladder in your condition?" he asked, knowing it must be dangerous.

"Like I always do. Carefully."

"Man, oh man, what am I going to do with you?" Jake gazed at her for a moment, shaking his head. She was bound and determined to give him a full head of gray hair before his fortieth birthday. He reached into his back pocket for his wallet, then pulled out a twenty-dollar bill. "Here, why don't you run down to that chicken place and get us something to eat, and I'll finish this."

Her mouth dropped open in surprise. "Since when do you know anything about wallpapering?"

He shot her a dark look. "It just so happens my place needed a lot of work when I bought it. I wallpapered two bathrooms and the kitchen." When she hesitated, he handed her his keys and prodded her toward the door. "Take the Jeep. I just put a full tank of gas in it."

"But I'm a mess."

"Use the drive-through window."

"Jake, I don't know. You've already done so much. I really didn't expect—"

"And make it fast. I didn't get lunch today."

He pushed her toward the door again before she could argue further.

Sammie returned to find two more strips of wallpaper in place. "Looks great," she said, then held up a large box of chicken. "Dinner's ready."

Jake ate quickly, then went back to work. Sammie tried to help him, but soon realized she was only being a bother. He wanted things done a certain way and became irritated when she did it differently.

Sammie cleaned the kitchen, straightened the rest of the apartment, put in a load of wash, then lay down on the sofa to rest a minute. Her feet were puffy. It felt so good to be off of them. Before long, she had fallen asleep.

It was almost two o'clock in the morning when Jake came out of the bedroom and found Sammie asleep on the couch in front of an old black-and-white movie. He walked over to the TV and turned it off. He hadn't realized it was so late. He'd been so determined to get the job done that he hadn't even looked at his watch.

He wondered if he should wake her or let her sleep where she was. She looked so comfortable, a throw pillow tucked beneath her head, hand wedged in between. The other hand lay across her rounded belly. He smiled. She would never believe how pretty she was. A thick strand of reddish-blond hair fell across her face. Her lips were slightly parted. Something stirred inside of him as he wondered what it would be like to kiss her. Sure, he'd kissed her on the cheek and forehead before, but he'd never tasted her lips or explored the inside of her mouth with his tongue. He was startled to realize just how badly he wanted to. Startled and confused. When had his feelings changed from simple friendship to blatant desire?

In the beginning he'd been compelled by guilt. If only he'd spent more time with Nathan, trained him better. But in his heart he knew he'd spent more time with Nathan than he had anyone else. What he should have done was work harder to get him out of narcotics.

Was it guilt that kept him coming back after all these months? Or was something else going on? He couldn't answer his own question.

Jake shook himself. It was late, and he knew he wasn't likely to find the answers while standing in the middle of her living room. He decided the sofa was not a good place for her to sleep because of its lack of support. He bent over and stroked her arm lightly. He was not surprised to find her skin smoother than anything he'd ever touched. "Sammie?"

She opened her eyes, then blinked twice as though bringing him into focus. She glanced around quickly. "Did I fall asleep?" He nodded, and she raised up. "What time is it?"

"Two A.M." He smiled proudly. "I finished the nursery. I even cleaned up the mess."

Her look softened. "Oh, Jake. What would I do without you?"

He tweaked her nose. When she looked at him like that, he felt it right in the pit of his stomach. "I'm not going to give you a chance to find out. Now, come on. You need to let me out so you can lock up behind me."

She paused. "Do you want to take the left-over chicken? That way you won't have to cook dinner tomorrow night. Or should I say to-night?"

He chuckled, amused that she could worry about food even when she was half asleep. "No, you need it more than I do," he said, then patted her belly softly. He decided he liked the way she felt. He leaned forward and kissed her on the cheek. A safe kiss. Something moved beneath his hand, and he jumped. "What was that?"

"The baby kicked." She looked pleased. She captured his hand in hers and held it in place. "Just a minute. You might feel it again."

He waited, thinking how no woman should be alone during this time in her life. Once again, he pushed his guilt aside. No amount of self-blame in the world would bring her husband back. Besides, she'd made it plain she didn't hold him responsible for Nathan's death. All he could do now was be there for her, share her excitements and disappointments, make her feel less alone.

Jake looked up suddenly. "I felt it again. Was that it?"

She nodded. "In the beginning it was only a flutter."

He smiled, squeezed her hand and raised it to his lips. "That's one lucky baby. To have a mother like you."

Her eyes registered doubt. "Do you really think I'm going to be a good mother?" she asked softly. "There's so much I have to learn. What if I can't do it?"

"You'll be a wonderful mother, Sammie," he told her as he let himself out.

Everybody in the department was talking about the bust when Jake walked in late the following morning. He'd played it down to Sammie, but he and his men had seized a small arsenal of weapons, not to mention enough crack-cocaine to keep a dealer in business for months.

"Congratulations, Jake," one of the men in the burglary unit said. "I hear you've been cleaning up our streets the past few days. Put a couple of punks in the hospital to boot. Who knows, you might make Atlanta a safer place to live after all."

Jake nodded as he made his way across the hall to his desk. "I'm damn sure gonna try." He was glad something had come through for him.

For three days the guys had been razing him for picking on grandmothers and babies. Although he hated to see the grandchildren separated from their maternal grandmother and put into foster care, he knew without a doubt they would receive better care.

Jake barely had time to sit down at his desk before a feminine voice pulled him away from his thoughts. Helen, the dispatcher, leaned across his desk. "I tried to call you last night. You must've been visiting the little widow."

He leaned back in his seat and regarded the woman. She was attractive as hell with blond hair and a knockout body. So what was the problem? "That's right. I wallpapered the nursery last night."

"Aren't you going a bit overboard on this, Jake? After all, the guys say you didn't even like her husband that much."

"What else do the guys say?"

She hesitated. "That you're doing it because you feel guilty over his death." When he didn't respond, she went on. "Look, it's none of my business, of course. You and I have only gone out once. But you shouldn't let this thing take over your life. You've been ignoring your friends for months." She sat on the edge of his desk. "A bunch of us are getting together for drinks and dinner at the Pit after work tonight. Why don't you join us? It'll be fun."

"Let me think about it."

She looked suddenly impatient. "I really need to know. My car is in the shop, and I don't have a way to get to the restaurant."

This meant she was supposed to be his date. Jake knew he should feel flattered, but he wasn't. "Okay, I'll go. But I can't stay out late. I have to work early tomorrow."

Ruby Johnson lived in a moderately priced ranch house less than a mile from Sammie's store. As Sammie made her way up the front walk, carrying a banana cream pie, she hoped she wasn't too late. Ruby had invited her to dinner, but Sammie had insisted on bringing something for dessert. She'd been craving banana cream for days. Unfortunately, she'd burned the meringue the first time she'd put it under the broiler, and had to scrape it off and start over. By the time the pie was presentable, she was late. She paused before the front door and knocked.

Ruby answered right away, giving her a smile that warmed her all over. "Good, you made it," she said, taking the pie. "We . . . I mean, I was getting worried. Come on in."

Sammie walked into the foyer, then followed Ruby to the living room, wondering why the other woman didn't go into the kitchen instead. She didn't have much time to think about it.

"Surprise!"

Sammie came to a startled halt at the sight of

the smiling women standing in the gaily decorated living room. A baby shower! She had never even suspected. She pretended to frown at Ruby. "Are you responsible for this?"

The woman grinned. Several others chuckled. "You know I am."

"Oh, Ruby." Sammie hugged her. "What a sweet thing to do."

"I need a hug too," an old friend named Marlene Henry said. She was married to a policeman. Sammie and Nathan had gone out with them a couple of times, and Marlene had done everything in her power to help Sammie in the months following his death.

"Hello, Marlene," she said, hugging her. "I've missed you."

"Then you're going to have to stop working so hard and meet me for lunch once in a while."

"You've gotten so faaaat," another woman said to Sammie. "What on earth happened?" Everybody laughed.

"She's obviously let herself go," another said.

"Too many Gummi Bears, I guess," Sammie replied. She frowned. "And you guys all look so skinny."

Ruby hurried into the kitchen to put the pie away, then returned to visit with the women and serve them each a cup of punch.

"Don't fill up," a woman named Janet Shields said. "We're taking you to dinner."

"Don't worry," Sammie reassured her. "I can

eat all day and night and still manage to find room for something else." More laughter.

After the women had visited for a while, Ruby insisted Sammie open her gifts. "This one's from me," she said. "And you have to open it first since I'm giving the shower."

Sammie took the rather large-size box and began tearing off the bows and paper. Ruby took it from her and placed the bow aside so she could reuse it. Sammie opened the present and found an infant's layette set inside, complete with outfits, booties, washcloth and towel. The women oohed and aahed. "Thank you, Ruby," Sammie said, reaching for her friend's hand and squeezing it. She knew the gift must've set her back. "I need all of this." She'd barely gotten the words out of her mouth before someone thrust another package at her.

Once Sammie'd opened her presents and passed them around, Ruby placed them on a library table nearby. There was a baby book, a plastic bathtub, a swing, a diaper bag, crib sheets and blankets, and a number of cotton gowns and sleepers. One of the women reached behind her chair and pulled out another large box and carried it over to her. She, too, was married to a policeman. "The guys at work took up a collection," she said. "They told me what they wanted to get you, and I picked it out for them."

Sammie unwrapped the gift and was surprised to find a very nice infant car seat inside.

She'd had her eye on a similar one and knew they were expensive. "Oh, how nice," she said, genuinely touched.

"Well, you know how policemen feel about kids and seat belts. But I saved the receipt so if it's not the brand you wanted, you can always exchange it."

"It's perfect," Sammie told her, feeling very close to tears. She had stayed away from the police department just as she had avoided being around many of her friends married to cops. It wasn't that she no longer wanted their friendship, she did. But she couldn't very well share her negative, fearful feelings with these women. They had married, like she had, for better or worse and in sickness and in health. They had borne children with their men. They didn't need Sammie telling them how dangerous their husbands' jobs were.

"And now, we're all going to dinner," Marlene said. "We've reserved a table at the Pit."

Sammie shouldn't have been surprised. The Pit was a favorite stomping ground for the police department and served the best barbecue in Atlanta. Both plainclothes detectives and uniformed officers often stopped off after work for a beer, and they took their families on weekends. Sammie had been there numerous times with Nathan, but not once since his death. "That sounds like fun," she said, not wanting to spoil the party for the rest of them. It was time she

started going to these places again. She pulled
Ruby aside on the way out the door and whispered, "You're not going to throw out the pie."

Ruby patted her hand. "No, dear. I'll bring it
to work tomorrow. You can have as much as you
like."

When the ladies arrived at the restaurant,
there was a waiting list. "It doesn't matter,"
Marlene said. "We have reservations for ten."

They were seated at a table in the back. At
Sammie's place was an arrangement of flowers
with a plastic stork in the middle, and the waitress told her she could take it home with her.
After ordering drinks, Sammie announced she
had to go to the bathroom.

"I'm going with you," Ruby said. "I don't
want you to trip and have that baby in the middle of this restaurant."

Together, they made their way past the bar
and toward the front of the restaurant. Sammie
saw him right away, standing with his back to
her, at least a head taller than everyone else. She
would have recognized him anywhere, the black
hair, the powerful shoulders draped in a snug
navy blue blazer. She paused, ready to call his
name over the crowd.

Ruby followed her gaze. "Isn't that—?"

"Yes," Sammie said, then stiffened when Jake
turned and saw her. Their gazes locked. Even
halfway across the room she felt as though he'd
touched her. Her gaze wandered to the person

next to him, a striking blonde. Her heart sank. The woman turned, and followed Jake's gaze. She frowned slightly when she saw Sammie before turning away.

"He's with somebody," Ruby whispered.

"Her name's Helen. They work together." Sammie forced herself to smile at Jake before she turned the corner and walked down a short hall to the rest rooms.

Ruby pushed the swinging door and held it open so Sammie could enter. "I wish you could see the expression on your face right now," she said. "Don't tell me there's nothing between you and Jake Flannery."

Sammie touched her cheeks. They felt hot. "I was just surprised," she said. "I wasn't expecting to—"

"See him with another woman?" Ruby asked knowingly. "Or to care so much that he was?"

Sammie disappeared inside a stall. Undaunted, Ruby kept talking. "You ask me, I think you're taking him for granted. He does all this stuff for you and what do you do?"

"I cook dinner for him every Thursday night," Sammie called back weakly.

"Anybody can do that. You've got to stop pretending that you're just friends. I'm telling you right now, that man wouldn't be doing the things he does for you if he wasn't crazy about you."

Sammie stepped out and made her way to the

sink where she washed her hands. "What do you propose I do, Ruby? March up to him, big belly and all, and confess my feelings?" She shook her head. "I'm about to give birth to another man's baby. What makes you think Jake is interested in taking on something like that?"

"If he loves you, he'll love your baby too."

"And what about the fact that Jake is in the same field as Nathan was? You know how I feel about police work."

"You can't spend the rest of your life being afraid."

"I'm not afraid, Ruby. But you know what I was like after it happened. I've worked hard to get to where I am now. I don't ever want to go through something like that again." She turned and made for the door.

Ruby sighed heavily as she followed. "Well, in all honesty I can't say that I blame you. It's just such a shame. You and Jake were made for each other."

Sammie wondered if she was right.

SIX

Sammie was ready and waiting when Jake arrived Sunday night to take her to their second prepared childbirth class. "How was the baby shower?" he asked as they made their way down the flight of stairs with him leading the way.

"You knew all along?" she said, studying his backside in a pair of snug jeans.

He tossed her a grin over his shoulder. "Marlene told me. But she didn't bother to tell me they were taking you to the Pit afterward."

She got the feeling he hadn't been pleased to see her. "I take it that was Helen I saw you with? I thought you said she wasn't your type."

"She's not. I sort of got railroaded into going."

Sammie paused at the bottom step. Her cheeks felt warm in the night air. There was a time when she hadn't minded knowing about the women in Jake's life. Not anymore. "Give me a break, Jake. I've got eyes. The woman looks like something out of a beauty pageant, big breasts and all."

He shrugged as he helped her into his Jeep, then got in on the other side. "Why do you care who I go out with?" he asked, watching her curiously.

"I don't," she said, trying to sound convincing. "I mean, I care that she's a nice person and all. I don't want you dating a shrew."

"I guess that sort of nips things in the bud for us then, huh?"

"I'm not a shrew, Jake," she said testily. "I just refuse to let anybody push me around. I won't be a doormat. You, of all people, should appreciate that in a woman. How many times have you said women need to know how to take care of themselves? Where I grew up, it was the first lesson we learned."

"You mean in the foster home?"

She glanced at him sharply. "How'd you know I grew up in a foster home?"

"Nathan mentioned it. Is that why you feel you have to be so tough?"

"Yes, if you must know the truth. There were a lot of kids there and not enough adults to go around. If you needed some attention, that was just too bad because odds were you weren't going to get it." She regarded him. "I'm not telling you this to make you feel sorry for me. I'm telling you so you'll understand. I had to learn to take care of myself, see to my own needs."

"What about Nathan?" he asked. "Didn't you need him?" When she didn't answer, he went on. "Or was Nathan the needy one in the relationship?" Jake looked over at her, but she was staring out the window. The look on her face told him she had no intention of telling him more than she had. She didn't have to. Knowing Nathan as he had, he was certain the relationship had left her wanting. Is that why she had been so eager for a baby? He wondered if he would ever know.

They were quiet on the ride, each of them caught up in their own thoughts. Still, it was a comfortable silence. They had spent enough time together that neither felt it necessary to fill that silence with nonessential chatter, like he had to do with Helen.

Jake pulled into the hospital parking lot and parked as close to the entrance as he could. As they walked toward the building, his hand at the small of her back, he noted the stares from people walking past them.

"They're wondering why I don't have Goodyear painted across my forehead," Sammie said miserably. "And why I'm not flying over some football field."

"You're not a blimp," Jake told her. "You happen to look very pretty tonight." It was the truth. She was wearing a skirt of brown and beige polka dots and a solid brown blouse. Her hair was pulled back with ivory combs, and she wore small gold loops in her ears.

She sighed heavily, as though she carried the weight of the world on her shoulders. "My ankles are swollen, my feet are swollen, and my hands are swollen. I'm never going to be able to wear real clothes again. I might as well sell my jewelry because none of my rings fit. I can't polish my toenails or shave my legs. The baby kicks all night and keeps me awake. I get indigestion every time I eat."

Jake paused at the door to the hospital. "Well, look at the good side. You still have your own teeth."

She put her hands on her hips. "This is not the time to joke. I'm ready to ask the doctor to induce labor."

"You have at least three weeks left. He's not going to induce. Besides, how many times have you told me first babies are usually late?"

"I'll die if it's late."

"You won't die. You just spent the last twenty minutes telling me how tough you are. How you're not a doormat and all that."

She touched his arm. "Jake?" She paused and glanced around as though she was about to share a great secret with him. "I sometimes come off sounding tougher than I really am," she admitted.

He acted surprised, and slapped one hand on his forehead. "You? No!"

She walked off in a huff. "Now, you're making fun of me."

He caught up with her, put his arm around her shoulder and pulled her close. "I'm not making fun of you." He was still trying to convince her of that fact when they arrived at the classroom. They spoke to several couples, all of whom were as anxious as Sammie to get it over with. Jake let them believe he was Sammie's husband as they bemoaned the fact that pregnancy seemed to last forever. One woman's feet were so swollen, she had resorted to wearing bedroom slippers. Finally, Sally walked into the room, and they moved to their seats.

"Don't get too comfortable," the instructor said. "We're going to tour the delivery room tonight."

"She won't make us go in while someone's having a baby, will she?" Jake whispered.

Sammie elbowed him in the side.

By the time the first half of class was over, everybody had gotten a good look at the labor and delivery rooms, and various equipment including the fetal monitor. Jake had only one question. "What are those silver thingamajigs at the bottom of the table?"

Sammie leaned close. "Stirrups." She glanced at him. He was turning his head this way and that as though trying to figure out what part

they played in the delivery process. Sammie
chuckled. "I think it'll be more fun if I let you
figure it out on your own."

"Be that way. I won't tell you where they
keep the painkillers."

They spent the rest of the class learning how
to breathe and relax through mild contractions.
Jake felt self-conscious. He glanced at the other
couples from time to time. They seemed to be
enjoying it, whispering to one another, sharing a
private smile or a brief kiss. Jake suddenly wondered what he was doing here. This wasn't his
baby. He wasn't even related, for Pete's sake.

He hated all this pretense.

"Jake?"

Sammie startled him from his thoughts.
"Huh?"

"You're supposed to be massaging my lower
back. Is something wrong?"

He shook his head and pressed against her
lower back. "No, I was just thinking about something."

"Helen?"

He looked disgusted with her. "No, I wasn't
thinking of Helen," he snapped so loudly, the
two couples nearest them looked up. They
glanced away quickly.

"Better watch it," Sammie whispered.
"They'll think you're having an affair while your
poor wife is pregnant."

His frown faded, and he chuckled. "Naw, I

think they've gotten to know you well enough that they'd understand completely."

She didn't look amused. "I can't wait until I'm in active labor and can tell you what I *really* think of you."

Jake had just pulled up in front of Sammie's apartment when a succession of high-pitched blips went off. She snapped her head around anxiously. "What the—?"

"Relax, it's just my beeper," he said, checking the number on it. "Mind if I use your phone?" He didn't want to tell her it was dispatch calling.

Inside, Sammie put on a pot of decaffeinated coffee while Jake dialed. "Hi, it's me," he said, when the woman picked up on the other end. "You got something for me?"

It had to be Helen, Sammie decided. She shot him a dark look but was quiet as he waited for his message and jotted down a number. "Yeah, thanks," he said. He hung up, then placed another call, this one long distance, before Sammie could question him. "May I speak to Mrs. John Flannery?" he asked. It was several minutes before he spoke again.

"Mom, it's me, Jake. What's going on?" He was quiet for a moment. "How serious is it?" When he hung up, he was frowning.

"What is it?" Sammie asked the second he put the phone down. She'd listened to the one-sided conversation long enough to know it wasn't good.

"My old man had a heart attack. He's in the hospital."

She gasped softly and put her arms around him. "Is he going to be okay?"

"They don't know yet." He wiped his hand across his forehead. "I've got to leave town for a few days. Do you think you'll be okay?"

"Sure. Is there anything I can do?" She hadn't seen him look this serious since Nathan died. At the same time, she dreaded his leaving.

He gave her a funny half-smile and patted her belly. "Just don't have the baby while I'm gone."

It was the longest week of Sammie's life.

She went to the doctor Monday afternoon, and listened to the baby's heartbeat but didn't get as excited as she usually did. She missed Jake, and he hadn't even been gone twenty-four hours yet. Her obstetrician patted her hand and told her it wouldn't be much longer now, and she wanted to tell him it wasn't the baby she was thinking about for once.

She ate dinner with Ruby and her husband on Wednesday, and Ruby said Sammie had a bad case of the lovesick blues.

"It's just gas," Sammie lied.

On Thursday, as she ate a lonely dinner by

herself, Sammie realized she had come to count on Jake more than she should have. Jake, who often surprised her by showing up at the shop to take her to lunch. Jake, who called just to see if she was feeling okay or dropped by unannounced in the evening with something sinfully delicious to eat. She figured the baby was responsible for half the weight she'd gained and Jake Flannery the other half.

Sammie longed to call the station and see if anyone had heard from him. But she didn't. Not only was she afraid Helen would answer, she felt uncomfortable for other reasons. She was Nathan Webster's widow, carrying his baby. What business did she have checking on another detective?

She and Jake were good friends, she argued with herself. She had a right to know if he'd made it to Jacksonville, Florida, okay, and whether his father had pulled through the heart attack. *Didn't* she have a right?

She picked up the phone.

She put it down.

Damn Jake for not calling her! Didn't he know she'd be worried out of her mind?

That was the problem with him, she told herself. He was just too damn independent for his own good. He was a confirmed bachelor, unaccustomed to answering to anyone. He came and went as he pleased, lived life on the edge and dared anyone to question him.

And he had accused her of not needing anyone. Who was *he* to talk?

So why was she allowing herself to feel this way about him? Why did she get all goose pimply every time he turned those dark eyes on her?

She was falling in love with Jake Flannery.

The knowledge made her drop her fork, and it clattered in her plate, startling her further. In love with Jake? When had it happened? *How* had it happened?

Oh, Lord, Ruby was right! It *wasn't* gas.

Sammie carried her plate to the sink. What was she going to do now, now that she knew the full extent of her feelings? How would she keep him from finding out? He spent most of his free time with her. He was her childbirth coach, for heaven's sake! He would know.

"He *can't* know," she told herself. Otherwise, he might feel compelled to return her affections, out of guilt if nothing else. She was Nathan's poor widow with a baby on the way. No, she would have none of that. Jake must never know her feelings for him had changed.

By Sunday afternoon, Sammie had resigned herself to the fact that she would have to attend the childbirth class alone. At the same time, she was annoyed with Jake for not calling. Being independent was one thing but being outright inconsiderate was another.

She was almost ready to leave when someone knocked at the door. Hoping it was Jake, she threw it open. He glared at her from the other side.

"You have a peephole, why don't you use it? Do you always just open the door without checking who is on the other side? Dammit, Sammie! How many times do I have to tell you these things?"

Her heart soared at the sight of him, and she resisted the urge to break out into a silly grin. She noted he held a suitcase. "Did you drive all the way back from Jacksonville just to tell me that?"

He stepped inside without waiting for an invitation. "I need to clean up," he said. "I can't go to the class smelling like this."

"You're going to the class with me?"

"What other class would I be going to?"

"I wouldn't know. You haven't called me all week. Mind my asking how your father is?"

"Better. He went home this morning." He paused. "Mind if I shower now?"

"Use the one in my room. The other one needs a liner."

She felt self-conscious as she led him into her bedroom. "You can put your suitcase on the bed if you like."

Jake paused in the doorway and took a look around. "It's frilly," he said, nodding toward the eyelet bedspread and dainty throw pillows. "Nathan didn't sleep on this stuff, did he?" He regretted it the moment he asked. What damn business was it of his anyway?

Sammie looked at him, and their gazes locked. She blushed and wondered why the question bothered her, wondered why he'd asked. "I changed it. After he died." She pointed to a door. "The bathroom is in there." She left the room and closed the door behind her.

Jake wasted no time stripping off his clothes and stepping into the shower. The bathroom was decorated much like the bedroom, with a delicate hand, strictly female. He grabbed the bar of soap and started to scrub, then rolled his eyes when he noted it was one of those perfumed moisturizer brands. He peeked outside the curtain, hoping to find a big bar of deodorant soap by the sink, but there was nothing.

She'd questioned him about not calling. Good. How many times had he picked up the phone to do just that, only to decide not to? Jake Flannery didn't check in with anybody. At least not a woman. He might check in with the captain or his men, but that was it.

What a crock!

Jake knew damn well that wasn't the reason he hadn't called. He hadn't called because he'd wanted to see if she would even notice. If she cared. As stubborn and independent as she was, he wanted to feel she missed and needed him just a little bit.

Had she?

Muttering a curse, he grabbed a towel, wrapped it around his waist and stepped out of the tub, leaving the shower running. He opened the bathroom door and made his way through her bedroom and into the living room. She was carrying a stack of neatly folded towels from the laundry room when she spied him, half-naked, dripping water all over the carpet. She jumped, dropping the towels.

"Oh, my," she said, taking in the massive chest and long muscular thighs. "What's wrong?"

"Do you have any real soap in the place?" he asked. "I can't use your sissy junk."

She tried not to stare. "There might be some in the other bathroom. Let me check." Leaving the towels on the floor, she hurried into the other room. When she returned, she was holding a sliver of deodorant soap. "This should be enough for now."

He looked doubtful as he disappeared into the bedroom. But not before Sammie noticed how nice his behind looked in a towel.

They were on their way to class soon after, arriving in the middle of a lesson on caring for the newborn, which included bathing and diapering. Several men volunteered to try their hand at the latter. One man held the diapered baby up for everyone to see, and the diaper slid right off the rubber doll into the bathtub, drawing laughter from the rest of the group. Afterward, they moved to the floor and practiced their breathing exercises.

When Sammie and Jake arrived back at her apartment, she asked him if he would walk with her for a while. "I haven't been sleeping well at night," she told him. "Maybe the fresh air and exercise will help."

"Sure," Jake said. "Take my hand. I wouldn't want you to stumble."

Slipping her smaller hand into his, Sammie found an easy pace and went with it. The night air felt good on her face. A soft breeze rustled the trees that surrounded the parking lot.

"I missed you while you were gone," she said after a minute, then held her breath for his reply.

He squeezed her hand. "I missed you too, babe. I was afraid you'd go into labor while I was gone."

She wondered if he knew how good it was to hear his voice again. "Is your dad going to be okay?" she asked.

"Yeah, he's going to make it. But he has to follow a strict diet and spend less time on the sofa in front of the TV set."

They continued walking. "Jake, I'm worried." He looked at her questioningly. "What if the pain of having a baby is too much for me, and I can't take it? What if I lose control?"

He squeezed her hand again. "You're not going to lose control. You're stronger than you think." His gaze grew serious. "Look what you've already been through."

"I wouldn't have been able to do it without your help."

He stopped and smiled down at her. "Is that your way of telling me you need me just a little?"

"I'm serious, Jake. What if I fall apart in there?"

He raised both hands to her shoulders. "I'm not going to let you fall apart. I'm going to be the best damn coach you ever had." He paused. "Besides, nobody is going to let you suffer that much pain. I'll see that they give you something." He released her shoulders and took her hand once more. She nodded as though he made sense. "There's something else we need to talk about," he said. "I've been giving it some thought lately."

"What is it?"

"I should probably move in with you for a while."

Sammie stopped walking. "Move in?"

"Surely you've thought about it. What happens if you go into labor in the middle of the night?"

"I call you."

"Something could happen, Sammie. I'd feel safer if I was with you. Besides, who is going to help you with your contractions until it's time to go to the hospital?"

"Where would you sleep?"

"I have a roll-away bed at home. I could put it up in the nursery." When she continued to look doubtful, he went on. "I'm not trying to threaten your sense of independence, Sammie. We're both gone during the day so we won't crowd each other. I'll try to stay out of your way in the evenings."

"It's not that," she said.

"Then what?"

She hesitated. How could she tell him she was falling for him and that spending more time with him would only make it worse when it was time to part? She had never learned to count on Nathan because Nathan always had so many needs of his own. Jake was like the rock she'd never had but wished she could cling to when life became too much. No, she couldn't tell him that. "I just don't want to be any trouble," she said instead. "You've already done so much."

He tweaked her nose. "Don't be silly. Now, I'd better get you to bed. I've got to get home and unpack and see if anything earth-shattering happened at headquarters while I was gone." He assisted her up the flight of stairs, then went in briefly for his things.

"I'll plan on moving in next Sunday after-noon."

"What if the baby's late?"

"Then we wait. You're talking to a man who has held stakeouts in broom closets and attics for days." He leaned over, kissed her softly on the lips, then started for the door. "Don't forget to lock up. And use the chain this time."

SEVEN

Jake arrived late Sunday afternoon with his suitcase and suit bag, a roll-a-way bed, and two plump pillows. He paused in the doorway and studied Sammie for a moment. Although he'd just seen her Thursday night, he sensed a change immediately.

"Something's different," he said.

"The baby dropped," she said proudly.

"Come again?"

"Remember, we talked about it in class? It's when the baby descends into the pelvis."

"So you're getting closer?"

She sighed. "I hope so. I go to the doctor tomorrow."

"You have my beeper number. You'll call the minute you know something?"

"Yes, Uncle Jake," she said. "Now, let me

help you get moved in. I made spaghetti for dinner."

He rolled the bed into the nursery and began putting it together. "You don't have to cook for me every night. I eat out a lot."

"I have to cook anyway. If you're here to eat, fine. If you're not, that's fine too."

"I'll split the grocery bill with you."

"I don't expect it. Do what makes you feel comfortable."

He chuckled. "You must be getting close. You're being agreeable."

She gave him a stern look. "Don't push it. I can change in a heartbeat."

"Don't I know it," he said, rolling his eyes, ignoring the dark look she shot him. "I'll be sure to always let you know where I am, just in case you pop . . . I mean, start labor."

"You do that, Jake. And I'll be sure to call right away. That way you can sit with me for the entire eighteen or twenty-four hours it takes for me to pop."

"We don't *know* you'll labor that long. You could have the kid in two hours and be done with it."

"That's not likely to happen, and we both know it. Do you want me to hang up your clothes for you?"

"I only have a couple of jackets. In case they make me attend a meeting at work. You know me. If I have to iron it or hang it up, I don't have any use for it."

She unzipped his suit bag and pulled out his navy blue blazer and a camel-colored jacket.

"I hope you don't mind, I had to give your number to a couple of guys at work. In case something comes up."

She looked up, her expression uncertain. "Didn't they think it was a little strange? Your staying here and all?"

"Not when I told them the reason."

"You actually told them?"

"You sound surprised."

"I wouldn't have thought—" She paused. "Never mind."

"You didn't think I'd tell anyone I was your childbirth coach?"

"Well, you do come across as being one of those macho guys who wouldn't be caught dead in a delivery room."

He looked at her. "Then you obviously don't know me very well, Sammie." When she didn't respond, he went on. "I work the streets. I've got a certain image to uphold. I've got to let the drug dealers and the pimps and the sickos know that I'm not going to take anything from them. I like to make them wonder if I'm not a little bit dangerous and crazy too." He paused. "I can't let them know I'm wallpapering a nursery or using massage therapy or listening to classical music in my spare time."

"I understand," she said at last. "And don't worry, your secret's safe with me. If anybody calls, I'll tell them you're cleaning your sawed-off shotgun or that you're out on the firing range catching bullets with your bare teeth."

He smiled. "Thanks."

"Now, would you like some spaghetti or would you rather go out back and forage in the dirt for your dinner?"

"Sammie?"

"Huh?"

"Forget what I said about being agreeable."

They ate an early dinner, then drove to their class where they practiced breathing exercises for strong contractions and learned how to fight the urge to push. Although it was only nine-thirty when they arrived home, Sammie was tired and ready for bed.

"I know you're a night owl," she told Jake. "Stay up as late as you like."

Jake finally turned off the television set around midnight. He went into the kitchen for a drink of water before going to his room, then froze at the sink when he heard a moan from Sammie's room. Without wasting a moment, he put the glass down, raced to her bedroom door and opened it.

Inside, he groped for the light switch, turned it on, and found Sammie thrashing in the bed. She cried out and bolted upright. Her forehead was creased in pain.

"Is this it?" Jake said, rushing to the closet for her bathrobe. All he could find was one of those furry numbers women wear on Christmas morning. She'd be hotter than hell. Oh well, it couldn't be helped. He took it from the hanger and hurried to the bed, along with a pair of fuzzy bedroom shoes that resembled twin Easter bunnies.

Sammie grabbed her leg and moaned again. "It's killing me, Jake."

He tossed the robe and shoes onto the bed and ran for her suitcase which was near the door. It was then he noticed he wasn't wearing his own shoes. "Oh, damn, let me find my sneakers," he muttered.

"Wait, Jake," she called out. "It's not what you think."

Jake came to a halt. "What?"

"It's just a charley horse." She continued to massage her calf.

"A charley horse? You mean, you're not having the baby?" He looked relieved as he returned to the bed. He began kneading her calf muscle. "Force the front of your foot upward . . . toward your knees."

"Ouch! I can't, it hurts."

"It's not going to go away until you do," he said sharply.

She flexed her foot and moaned some more. "It's easing up, I think," she said after a moment. "Okay, it's gone."

He continued to rub her leg. "You scared the hell out of me, you know that?"

She moved the robe aside, frowning when she saw it was her winter one. The bedroom shoes had been a gag gift from Ruby for her last birthday, and she almost shuddered at the thought of being caught in them. "You thought I was in labor?"

"That surprise you?" he said. "What would *you* think if an almost-nine-month-pregnant woman started moaning in the middle of the night? Do you have these often?"

"Several times a week."

"You know what it's from, of course."

"I know you're going to tell me whether I want to hear it or not."

"It's from standing on your feet all day. You're going to have to give up working for a while, Sammie."

"Give up working?"

"It's for your own good."

"But what would I do all day?"

He pretended to think. "I got it. Why not rest?"

"I'd be bored out of my mind. I'd eat all the time."

"You already eat all the time."

"That's not funny, Jake." She paused in thought. "I'll cut down on the grooming. That way I won't have to stand so much."

"What about all you do around here?" he

asked, remembering she was an immaculate housekeeper. "Maybe you should cut down on that too. I could do the vacuuming."

She nodded thoughtfully. "We might have to eat a few frozen dinners."

"Hey, I can eat a peanut butter sandwich for dinner. It makes no difference to me." It was only then that he realized he was still rubbing her leg. Caressing it, actually. He quickly released it, hoping she hadn't noticed. He stood and shoved his hands deep in his pockets. "I'd better let you get some sleep," he said. "Will you be okay?"

She nodded and scooted beneath the cover. "Thanks, Jake. As always, you're a lifesaver. What would I do without you?"

Those words echoed in his head as Jake closed the door behind him and made his way to the other bedroom.

Jake arrived at the apartment several days later and found Sammie taking the place apart. Literally. He walked into the kitchen and found her standing on a stepladder in shorts and a baggy shirt, pulling canned goods out of a cabinet.

"What the hell are you doing?" he demanded, thinking she had surely lost her mind this time.

She turned around. "Hi, Jake," she said, giving him a big smile. "We were slow at the shop today so I took the afternoon off, hoping I could catch up on a few things here. You know, once the baby comes, I won't have time for thorough cleaning."

He had only two things on his mind at the moment. Yes, he should be able to catch her if she fell, and, no, he couldn't remember when he'd seen shapelier legs. He coughed. "What are the potted plants doing outside?"

"I bought new potting soil at the store today so I could change them."

"You're going to change the soil in your plants?"

"That's right. The old soil has been in there for years. All the nutrients are gone. Look, Jake, I don't mean to be rude, but I really do have a lot to do. Why don't you go make yourself comfortable on the sofa and watch the news."

"Not until you come down off that stepladder." When she opened her mouth to protest, he went on. "You're not supposed to be climbing up on things. If you want the cabinets cleaned out, though I can't imagine why, *I'll* do it."

"You won't do it as good as I will."

"Well, I'm all you got, kid, so you'll just have to deal with it. Find something else to do while I change into something sloppy." He noted her raised eyebrow. "Okay, something sloppier."

"I'll clean out the refrigerator," she said.

He thought she looked excited over the prospect, and he was almost afraid to leave her, even for a minute. "I'll be right back."

Jake hurried into the spare bedroom and dialed Marlene Henry's number on the portable phone near his bed. She answered on the first ring.

"Marlene, this is Jake," he said. "You know quite a bit about babies, right?"

The woman on the other end of the line laughed. "I have three children, if that means anything."

"Good. I assume you know I'm helping Sammie Webster through her pregnancy and all that."

"I'd heard you were going to be her childbirth coach. I thought that was mighty decent of you considering she has no family."

"Well, I'd rather you keep this conversation between us," he said, knowing Marlene knew many of the other wives and could ruin him if she wanted.

"Okay, Jake, mum's the word."

"What I want to know is, do pregnant women ever start acting kind of crazy for no apparent reason?"

She chuckled. "I think it comes with the territory, why?"

"Sammie has gone on a cleaning spree. It's like she can't help herself. The apartment's in shambles, and she's giving no indication of stopping."

Marlene laughed out loud this time. "She hasn't gone crazy, Jake. She's just nesting."

"Come again?"

"It's something women go through right before they have the baby. She probably hasn't had a whole lot of energy lately and now she's got this sudden burst, and she wants to get everything done at once."

"So I shouldn't try to stop her?"

"No. It's not dangerous. Just don't let her move any heavy furniture. If you're lucky, she'll get it all put back into place before she goes into labor."

When Jake returned to the kitchen in his old clothes, he found Sammie pulling everything out of the refrigerator. She glanced up at him. "Would you shampoo the carpets if you were me?"

He didn't hesitate. "No, I definitely would *not*," he said, knowing he'd get stuck doing it. "And I'll tell you why."

She waited.

He had to think a minute. "Because of all the chemicals they put in the cleaner, that's why," he said at last. "It's not just soap like they lead you to believe, Sammie. You have no idea what they put in that stuff . . . probably toxic . . . you don't want to bring a new baby home to that."

"You're right," she said, convinced. "Forget that idea."

He tried not to let his relief show.

"Besides, that'll give me time to pull all the curtains down so I can wash and iron them."

They cleaned through the evening. When Jake fell into bed shortly before midnight, he was exhausted, but he awoke the next morning and found Sammie rarin' to go. He could not remember when he'd been so glad to go to work.

He called the shop that afternoon and was told by a concerned Ruby that Sammie was in the process of cleaning the dog cages.

"Oh, well, it's all part of being pregnant," Jake told the older woman as though he were an expert. "I just hope she wears down before long or I'm going to have to go into the hospital with her."

Two days later, Sammie's energy left as quickly as it had come, but not before Jake had washed and waxed their vehicles and polished the chrome till it shone like a new coin. He arrived home to find her taking a nap on the sofa. She didn't look well.

"You okay, sweetheart?" he asked, automatically putting a hand to her forehead.

She sighed heavily. "I had a tough day. I think all that cleaning really did me in. How about we take it easy tonight?"

Jake wanted to weep. "Well, I did have a few more items to take care of, but I suppose it can wait. Why don't I make us something simple to-night and we'll veg-out on the sofa?"

She nodded. "You got yourself a deal, mister."

Jake was so tired, he didn't hear the noise at first. Someone in the apartment? He bolted up-right in the bed and listened. It was coming from Sammie's room. Was she pacing? He rubbed his eyes and blinked, trying to get the sleep out. A gray, pre-dawn light filtered through the win-dow, and he could make out the crib against the wall. He climbed out of bed and stumbled toward the closet where he found his jeans wad-ded into a ball on the shelf. He stepped into them and hurried past the living room to her door. He knocked gently. "Sammie, are you okay?" Probably just another leg cramp, he thought. It amazed him how concerned he grew over the smallest thing.

When she opened the door, she was smiling. "Guess what?"

She looked so pretty that he couldn't resist smiling back. It didn't matter that she had inter-rupted his sleep or caused him to worry. He was simply glad to see her. "What?" he asked.

"I'm in labor, that's what."

EIGHT

He stared at her, thinking he had surely misunderstood her. "Are you sure? How do you know it's not leg cramps?"

She gave him a funny look. "Don't you think I'd know the difference? I've been having contractions since two o'clock this morning."

"And you didn't wake me?"

"There was nothing you could do, and I figured you needed your rest. Besides, I feel great. All my energy is back."

That comment made him wonder if he was going to have to clean the apartment until they went to the hospital. "But we haven't graduated from our childbirth class yet," he said in a voice that did not resemble one of Atlanta's top detectives.

Sammie slapped her forehead with the palm

of her hand. "Gee, if only I had thought about that *before* the contractions began."

Jake realized he was acting like an idiot. He had to get control. He checked for his wrist-watch and found he wasn't wearing it. It was hard to look like a man in control when you were standing there half-naked. "Okay, how far apart are your contractions?" he said, becoming all business.

"About seven minutes apart, lasting thirty-five to forty seconds."

He raked his hands through his hair. "Okay, what does that mean exactly?"

She looked amused. "It means you have plenty of time to shower and have breakfast. You may want to call the office."

"Call the office? Right. Okay. Maybe I'll do that after my shower."

"Good. In the meantime, I'll put on a pot of coffee. It looks like you need a cup."

Jake was in and out of the shower in three minutes flat, half-afraid he'd find Sammie giving birth in the middle of the kitchen floor. He threw on some clothes and hurried out of his room, following the smell of frying bacon. "How can you think of eating at a time like this?" he said.

She looked up. "It's not for me, silly; it's for you. You're going to need to keep up your strength. No telling how long this will go on."

She sounded so calm. He hated that. He was

the one who was supposed to be cool and level-headed. "Mind if I pour myself a cup of coffee?"

She didn't look up from the stove. "You've been around here long enough to know you don't have to ask."

He poured his coffee and sipped it slowly, watching her out of the corner of his eye. She lifted the bacon out of the skillet, then moved the pan aside so the grease could cool.

"Stop staring at me, Jake. The baby isn't going to just fall out in the middle of the kitchen floor." Even as she said it, she tensed and moved her hands to her belly.

"Are you having one?"

She nodded, closed her eyes, and took a deep breath.

He watched, fascinated and anxious at the same time. She was beautiful, standing there with the sun streaming in through the window. Beautiful and more feminine than anything he'd ever seen. After a moment she relaxed.

"Is it over?"

"Uh-huh. It wasn't bad. How do you want your eggs?"

The last thing he wanted to talk about was how he wanted his eggs. "We should go to the hospital."

"Don't be ridiculous. It's much too soon."

"Yeah, but you've heard those stories where the women have one contraction, then, wham!" He punched one palm with a fist.

She looked amused. "Wham?"

"Yeah, the baby pops out before they know what hit them. That's why women are always having babies in the backseat of some car or in the produce section of the grocery store."

"Well, I don't need anything from the store today so we're safe."

"You're not at all anxious, are you?" he asked, irritated that she could remain calm when he could feel his guts shaking.

She closed the distance between them and kissed him lightly on the cheek. He smelled of soap and after-shave. His shirt was slightly wrinkled but clean. The scar on his jaw made him look like the worst kind of rogue. Still, he was sexier than any man had a right to be. "Nor should you be anxious," she said.

He gazed into her green eyes and found only excitement. This was her day, the day she had been waiting months for. He wasn't going to blow it for her by being scared. Childbirth was no big thing these days, nothing was going to happen to her. He realized suddenly that he had been afraid of losing her, if not physically then emotionally. It had been just the two of them for so long. Would she still need him after the baby came? He smiled and returned the kiss, pressing his lips briefly against hers. "You're right," he said.

She looked pleased. "Now, tell me how you want your eggs. I have to call Ruby. And I suppose Nathan's parents as well," she added, although she didn't sound excited at the prospect.

The contractions continued on and off for the next couple of hours. Jake could tell Sammie was growing frustrated that more progress wasn't being made. "Let's go for a drive," he said, thinking it would take her mind off her contractions and the impending labor. "You know that snow-cone place near the mall that has something like a zillion flavor varieties? It won't hurt you to have one of those." He knew she wasn't supposed to eat anything, but surely a simple snow cone wouldn't create any problems.

"We'll need to take my bags," Sammie told him. "They're in my room."

"Sure. No problem." He followed her into her bedroom and found her bags on the bed. He looked at her. "You're taking all of this?"

"I need it," she said defensively. "The suitcase has all my nursing gowns and underclothes. That other bag has the supplies we're supposed to bring with us into labor."

"Okay, okay," he said, picking up the bags. "It's just . . . you're only going to be there for a few days, for Pete's sake."

They were on their way in minutes, heading for the snow-cone stand. They pulled up in front and saw that it didn't open for several more hours.

"Oh no!" Sammie cried, gripping the door handle until her knuckles turned white.

Jake offered her a funny look. "Gee, I know you're disappointed, honey," he said, backing out of the parking area. "I'm sorry."

"This is terrible!" she wailed. "I don't know what to do."

Jake figured she must've really had her heart set on a snow cone the way she was carrying on. "It's not the end of the world, sweetheart. We'll come back after the baby is born. I promise."

"It's not that, Jake," she cried. "My water just broke." She looked apologetic. "All over your seat."

He froze. "Are you sure?"

She was getting tired of him asking that question. "It's not something you can easily confuse with something else."

They made the fifteen-minute ride to the hospital in record time, with Jake reaching over to pat Sammie on the knee every minute or so. It worried him that she was so quiet, so withdrawn, when only an hour before she had been excited and in a good mood. "How far apart are they?" he asked, as he pulled into the emergency entrance.

"Four minutes. Lasting almost sixty seconds."

Jake stopped the car, climbed out, and hurried around to her side to help usher her into emergency. The admissions process was brief since Sammie had preadmitted herself. A plastic band was fastened around her wrist, she was seated in a wheelchair and taken to labor and delivery where she would be prepped. Jake used the few minutes to move the car and bring in her bags.

When he arrived at the nurses' station in labor and delivery, he was told to wait outside the door to Sammie's room until they finished with her. He was anxious, wondering what was taking so long. Finally, the door opened and a tall, big-boned nurse stepped through, wearing a name tag that read Mrs. Ratchet. Jake gave her a sheepish smile.

"No, Mr. Webster, I'm not related to the nurse who played with Jack Nicholson in *One Flew over the Cuckoo's Nest.*"

He looked relieved. "I guess you get that all the time, huh?"

"All the time. You may go in now, Mr. Webster. I've already performed your wife's lobotomy, I mean, prep."

Jake watched her go, a smirk on her face. Just what he needed right now, a comedian. He stepped into the room and found Sammie sitting on the edge of the bed wearing a hospital gown. "You okay?" he asked.

She nodded. "My contractions are stronger. Nurse Ratchet says I should walk around. It'll take my mind off the discomfort and speed things up."

Jake nodded dumbly, then snapped into his

coach role. "That's a good idea, honey," he told her. "Why don't we do that?"

Sammie was quiet as he ushered her out into the hall. She didn't speak until they were alone. "The pain is really starting to build, Jake," she whispered. "I don't know if I can do this."

"Sure you can. You've been doing great so far—" He paused when she stopped walking and tensed. "Are you having one?" She nodded and he checked his wristwatch. "Okay, take a deep breath."

They went through their breathing exercise. Sammie cooperated fully with what he told her to do. Piece of cake, Jake thought.

Two hours later, he changed his mind.

"Why don't you take a shower, honey?" he suggested, when nothing he said or did seemed to help. They were back in the labor room where he was showing her old card tricks and trying to get her interested in a game of poker.

"I don't want a shower," Sammie said between gritted teeth. "And I don't want to watch any more stupid card tricks." She swiped her hand across the bed table, and the cards flew in a dozen different directions.

Jake arched one brow. "Okaaay, no more cards." He snapped his fingers. "I know. I'll turn on some music." He reached into the bag near her bed and brought out the portable tape player.

"I don't feel like listening to music." She'd

barely got the words out of her mouth before a contraction hit. "Oh, damn, they're coming closer and closer together."

"Don't tense up, baby," he said. "Take a deep breath and start breathing rapidly." He showed her how. When she refused to follow, he knew he was in trouble. She moaned aloud, a sound that split his heart in two. Her contraction peaked, and she grabbed the bed covers and cried out. "I'm calling the nurse," Jake said and raced out of the room.

Nurse Ratchet wasn't far. She hurried into the room in her efficient way and examined Sammie, then smiled satisfactorily. "She's dilated eight centimeters. I'll put a call in to her doctor. Mrs. Webster, you're moving quite fast. It won't be long now." She'd barely gotten the words out of her mouth before another contraction hit.

"You've got to give her something," Jake said, as the contraction steadily worsened. Sammie looked as though she was going to lose it.

"I can't give her anything without doctor's orders," the nurse said, going out of the room.

Jake followed. "Then find her damn doctor and tell him I said to give her something," he snapped.

Nurse Ratchet regarded him coolly. "You should be in there helping your wife, Mr. Webster. Not badgering me."

"My wife has been in labor since two o'clock this morning. She's had it."

"I'll have to see what the doctor says," she said, dismissing him.

Jake could see she wasn't taking him seriously. "Look lady, I'm a cop. I own a gun."

Jake returned to the labor room and found Sammie digging through her suitcase. "Get me out of here," she demanded, rising up from the bed. "I've had enough."

Jake saw the fear in her eyes. "Sammie, you can't leave," he said, wondering if she'd lost her mind. They hadn't prepared him for this stage of labor. "The baby's almost here, honey. They're calling your doctor. It's almost time to go to the delivery room." He reached for her suitcase and stuck it under the bed and out of sight.

"I can't go through with it, Jake," she said, her eyes tearing. "I'm so tired."

He put his hands on her shoulders. "But you've been doing so well. Look how strong you are, Sammie. Look what you've already done. Most women would have given up long ago. You went through your whole pregnancy alone."

She sniffed. "Don't be ridiculous. I was never alone. I always had you."

Nurse Ratchet returned with a needle. "Mrs. Webster, I'm going to give you something that will relax you."

"I don't want to relax. I want to leave this place." She snapped her head up suddenly as she was overcome with a contraction. "I want to . . . push."

"Don't push!" the nurse said, then showed her how to breathe to keep from pushing. "Please help me get her flat on the bed," she told Jake as soon as the contraction had passed.

They finally coaxed Sammie into a reclining position so the nurse could give her an injection.

"How long before it knocks me out?" Sammie said wearily.

"It won't knock you out, dear, but it'll take some of the edge off."

"That's not good enough." She turned to Jake. "Just shoot me and put me out of my misery."

The doctor arrived ten minutes later and checked Sammie. He was impressed with her progress. "You ready to have that baby, Sammie?"

She was in the throes of another contraction. "I don't care if you have to perform a C-section," she managed. "Just get it out."

The doctor winked at the nurse. "Let's go to the delivery room."

Stephanie Marie Webster was born an hour later, weighing a robust eight pounds and two ounces. As Jake held the infant he knew he would never be the same.

"She looks just like you, Mr. Webster," one of the delivery room nurses said. He was glad Nurse Ratchet hadn't joined them.

Jake and Sammie exchanged private smiles. "Yeah, I think so too," he told the woman.

Once they took the baby away to clean and check her, Jake was shown where to go to get out of the sterile garments he'd worn into the delivery room. By the time he arrived back in the labor room, they'd already changed Sammie into a fresh gown and put her in bed. She gazed back at Jake, a sleepy smile on her face. "Well, what do you think?"

He wondered if he would ever view women in the same light. The miracle of birth had touched him like no other event ever had. He felt less cynical about life and the people in it. "Congratulations," he said, taking one of her hands in his. "You did it."

She moved his hand to her cheek. "Correction. *We* did it." Then, still holding his hand, she drifted off to sleep.

When Jake walked into Sammie's hospital room the next morning with fresh flowers and a gigantic teddy bear, he found her nursing the baby. "Ooops, I can come back later," he said.

"Don't be silly," she told him. "You've seen every other part of my anatomy, don't get shy on me *now*!" She smiled. "Are those flowers for me?"

He held them up. "What, these? No, they're for the baby. I thought the poor kid was going to end up being born in the parking lot when I walked into the labor room and found you digging for clothes in your suitcase."

She gave him an apologetic look. "Was I difficult?"

He leaned over and kissed her forehead. "You were wonderful." He gazed down at the sucking infant. Her fist lay against Sammie's breast. He was touched by the sight. He stroked the baby's cheek, and she started sucking faster. They both laughed, and he felt more comfortable in the intimate surroundings.

"If everything goes okay, they're releasing me tomorrow," Sammie told him.

Jake looked up quickly. "So soon?"

"My doctor doesn't believe in keeping new moms in the hospital any longer than he absolutely has to. He says Stephie and I are in excellent health."

"Stephie?"

"That's what I'm calling her. I figured the name Stephanie was much too pretentious for such a tiny baby." She smiled down at the infant who'd fallen asleep at her breast. Suddenly, she glanced up. "Oh, by the way. Do you have any plans for tonight?"

He shrugged. "Nothing that I can't get out of."

"The hospital gives new parents a nice dinner on their last night here. It's at seven. Would you like to come? You don't have to stay long."

He was amused at her attempts to ask him for a semidate. He couldn't resist teasing her. "Are you sure there's no one else you'd rather ask, now that you've gotten your figure back?"

She chuckled softly. "Believe me, my figure is *not* back yet. The basketball is gone, but there's a lot of baby fat that ended up on me instead of the baby." She paused, and her look grew tender. "Besides, there's no one I'd rather go with than you."

Nathan's mother was a petite redhead who dressed in smart two-piece suits and didn't look like she belonged with the burly ex-policeman to whom she'd been married almost forty years. As they walked into Sammie's room during visiting hours that evening, they both had tears in their eyes. Amanda Webster leaned over and kissed Sammie on the forehead.

"The baby is beautiful," she announced. "She looks just like Nathan."

"You really think so?" Sammie hadn't been able to find any resemblance, but she wasn't going to tell the Websters as much.

"Hello, Sammie," Burt Webster said, giving her a brief hug. "Amanda's right. I've never seen a prettier baby. You've named her?"

"Stephanie Marie. I was told that was my mother's name."

"How are you feeling?" Amanda asked.

Sammie laughed. "Pretty good compared to how I was feeling this time yesterday. Labor seemed to drag on, but I understand it wasn't as long as some of them."

"Remind me to tell you about my labor with Nathan one of these days," the older woman said, rolling her eyes. She stopped laughing, and her face turned sad. Burt put his arm around her. The room was quiet.

Sammie was uncomfortable. Although there had been brief phone calls between them since Nathan's death, she had avoided spending time with them, just as she assumed they'd avoided her. But surely they were happy she was still carrying on a part of their son.

"We want to know what your immediate plans are," Amanda asked once the uncomfortable moment had passed.

"All I plan to do is go home and get acquainted with my new daughter," Sammie said.

Amanda smiled. "Burt and I have discussed it, and we would like for you to stay with us for a few weeks. You could stay in Nathan's old room."

"We'd love to have you," Burt said. "That way you'll have some help during those first days when you're so tired."

Sammie looked from one to the other. They were undoubtedly sincere. But the thought of sleeping in Nathan's room and rehashing his death and the funeral and their grief afterward wasn't what she needed at this point. She had already done her grieving, had finally come to terms with her loss, thanks to Jake. What she wanted to do now was celebrate the birth of her daughter, not mourn the loss of her husband.

"I don't know," Sammie said after a moment. "I was really looking forward to settling in at home. Besides, all Stephie's stuff is there and I only have a few weeks before I have to go back to work."

"That's another thing," Burt said, reaching into his back pocket and bringing out an envelope. "Amanda and I didn't really know what to get you so we decided to give you cash instead. I think you'll find this more than enough to tide you over so you don't have to rush back to work."

Sammie opened the envelope. Inside was a cashier's check for ten thousand dollars. Her mouth dropped open.

"We kept an insurance policy on Nathan," Amanda said. "We'd like to give part of it to you now, and the rest when Stephanie is ready for college. We've already set up a trust fund. Burt can explain it to you later."

Sammie had tears in her eyes. "I don't know what to say," she said. "I never expected this."

Burt patted her hand. "We know you didn't. We would have given it to you sooner, but it took forever to get through the red tape. Once we finally got it, we decided to wait and give it to you when the baby came."

Amanda took Sammie's other hand. "I just want you to know one thing," she said. "I know Nathan could be stubborn and pigheaded at times . . . he always wanted things his way and all, but we offered to cash in this policy a few years back so the two of you could buy a house. Nathan told us to keep it in case anything ever happened to him."

Sammie shook her head, touched that Nathan had been concerned about her future. "I don't know what to say," she admitted. "Nobody has ever done this sort of thing for me." She reached for Amanda and Burt, and the three of them hugged. And cried some more.

Jake picked that particular moment to show up. He took one look at the situation and backed away, but not before Sammie spotted him.

"Jake, come in," she said, wiping tears from her face, looking embarrassed. He paused in the doorway.

He recognized Nathan's parents from the funeral. "Am I interrupting something?"

Burt stepped forward and held his hand out. "Jake, it's been a while," he said. "How are you?"

Jake shook the man's hand, and they exchanged pleasantries. Amanda crossed the room and hugged him. "We want to thank you for all you've done for Sammie these months," she said.

"I'm afraid Burt and I weren't much help to her." Her eyes clouded. "We've had a tough time bouncing back after Nathan's death."

Jake shifted uncomfortably. "Well, that's certainly understandable," he said, wishing he'd waited another hour before coming to see Sammie. He was clearly out of place. Nathan should have been here, not him. Was that what the Websters were thinking? Were those smiles for real or were they trying to mask their resentment?

"Is something wrong, Jake?" Sammie said, noting his discomfort.

He checked his wristwatch. "Actually, I'm supposed to be somewhere in half an hour. I just wanted to check in and see if you needed anything."

Sammie was irritated with his reluctance to stay. Why was he acting so weird? Was it because of the Websters or was he tired of hanging around her hospital room? Perhaps he felt he'd done his part now that the baby was born, fulfilled his obligation. "You shouldn't feel compelled to come every time they have visiting hours, Jake. I know you mean well, but I certainly don't expect it."

If he was uncomfortable before, it was nothing compared to now. What had happened to her in the short time he'd been away? "You'll call if you need anything?" he said. "If I'm out, just leave a message on my answering machine."

"Talk to you later, Jake," she said formally.

He didn't draw an easy breath until he'd exited the hospital and was making his way across the parking lot to his Jeep. Jake unlocked his door and climbed in, then sat there in the darkness for a moment. He'd made a damn fool of himself rushing into the hospital room as though he was the new father, as though he had a right to stand by Sammie's side and beam. The Websters probably thought he was crazy. Is that why Sammie had turned cool on him? Had he embarrassed her?

Stephie was not his daughter, and he had no right to pretend otherwise. He had served his purpose. He had befriended Sammie after her loss and tried to support her during the difficult months following. He had coached her through the delivery as she'd asked. Now she was beginning a new chapter in her life. It was only natural that she would want to relinquish her ties with the past and look to the future.

It was time he got on with his own life.

But there was still that dinner to get through.

NINE

The room was small and cozy, with only five or six tables draped in white. Jake selected one near the window and wished he could have thought of a plausible excuse for not being there. Of course, things were always coming up at work. It wouldn't have been out of the ordinary if he'd had to stay late. But as much as he dreaded facing Sammie, he couldn't stand the thought of her not having someone to dine with her on this special evening.

While Jake waited for her, another couple strolled in and took a table on the other side of the room. Jake envied the guy. He had a right to be there. He wasn't just filling in for the real father.

Stop feeling sorry for yourself, he thought.

Sammie appeared a few minutes later, wearing a blue-and-white polo-style dress and navy

pumps. Jake stood and waited for her approach.
He forced himself to smile. He would not let his
own discomfort ruin her evening.

"You look very pretty," he said, going to her
side of the table and pulling her chair out for
her. He leaned over and kissed the top of her
head. An innocent kiss. Brotherly. But he
couldn't help but notice her hair smelled of wild-
flowers.

"Sorry I kept you waiting," she said, smiling
as well. "You don't look so bad yourself. Are
those new jeans?"

He looked embarrassed with the compliment. "Yeah, I keep them around in case I have
to be in a wedding or something."

She chuckled as she took in the freshly
starched brown-and-peach shirt and wrinkle-free
camel-colored jacket. "I'm impressed." Their
gazes met for the first time. "Frankly, I'm surprised you recognized me with makeup," she
said. "I really let myself go this past week."

"I hadn't noticed," he told her, then wondered if it had sounded corny. It was hard to joke
with her when he felt so tense. The old camaraderie was missing.

A smiling waitress appeared with two glasses
of sparkling grape juice. "We have London Broil
or Flounder Delmar on the menu tonight," she
said. "It comes with a spinach salad and twice-
baked potato. Which would you like?"

Jake ordered the steak and Sammie the fish.

When the waitress was gone, she turned to him. "I was afraid you weren't going to show up tonight. Mind telling me why you acted so strange this afternoon?"

"You shouldn't have to ask," he said. "I felt uncomfortable with Nathan's parents."

"Why? Have they said or done anything to offend you?"

"It's nothing like that. I just feel like I'm in the way. I know they're probably thinking how unfair it is that I'm the one in your hospital room and not their son."

"Oh, so now you're a mind reader."

"Haven't there been times you wished I was the one who got shot that day instead of Nathan?"

She looked offended. "What a terrible thing to ask."

"You would be only human to feel that way."

"You think that's the way the Websters feel as well?" she said.

"Could you blame them? Nathan was younger than me . . . had a family and all."

"We're back to the old guilt routine, aren't we, Jake? That's what this is all about. When are you going to let it go?"

His jaw became hard. "You asked me why I felt uncomfortable with Nathan's parents, and I told you."

"Well, you listen to me, Jake Flannery. I never once wished it had been you that died instead of Nathan. How you can even think that after what we've been through is beyond me, and if you're going to continue this morbid conversation at what is supposed to be my celebration dinner, then I'm going to have to excuse myself."

She started to get up but Jake stopped her, leaning forward and placing a restraining hand on hers. "I'm sorry," he said. "Please don't go."

She relaxed. "Then I'd appreciate it if we could talk about something else."

"Okay, how about I make a toast?" He reached for his glass and raised it. "To prepared childbirth," he said.

She raised her own glass, thankful for the change of subject. She had been thinking of Nathan on and off all day. Thinking of him and feeling bad that he hadn't lived to see his daughter. Wishing things had been different between them. She had decided it was normal to expect a certain amount of sorrow on this occasion, but that didn't mean she was slipping back into her grieving mode. She *couldn't* grieve. She had to think of the baby. She toasted Jake's glass. "I don't think you're *ever* prepared for childbirth," she said, her smile giving away none of her thoughts.

They each took a sip of their juice. Jake set his glass down. "So when are you going to do it again?"

She arched both brows. "Have another baby? Hmmm. I think I'll adopt next time."

"I thought it was neat," he said.

"Neat? That's because you weren't the one on the delivery table."

"I have a new respect for women," he confessed. "I will never think of them as the weaker sex."

The mood was considerably brighter, and she welcomed it. "I never knew you did."

He winced. "Only once when I had to change a lady's tire for her. It would never have crossed my mind otherwise."

She laughed. "You're a lying dog, Jake. I know you feel men are superior."

"Not after yesterday. I'd rather be shot than go through what you went through." He regretted his word choice the instant he said it, but she chose to ignore it. He was thankful when the waitress brought their salads.

By the time their meal arrived, they were both relaxed with each other. Just like old times. Sammie described her day with Stephie, and Jake talked about his day at work. It wasn't until after their plates had been carried away and the coffee was served that Jake asked the question he'd been wanting to ask all evening.

"You never told me how your visit went with Nathan's parents?"

She hesitated. "They were very sweet and apologetic for all the months they avoided me." She told him about the insurance check, and he was genuinely happy for her. "I won't have to rush back to work," she said. "I've already called the groomer, and she can stay as long as I need her."

"That's great," he told her. "I know you didn't want to have to go back so soon." Actually, he'd wanted to loan her the money himself so she could stay home with the baby longer, but he hadn't been able to come up with a way of doing it without offending that stubborn independent streak in her. He was glad the problem had been solved, but it irritated him that he hadn't made the offer sooner. He wanted to be the one she could count on.

"They want me to come stay with them for a while," Sammie said after a moment.

He wasn't surprised. "Are you?"

She looked sad. "I don't want to. I know I should probably consider it since I can't drive for a couple of weeks and the thought of being alone with a new baby terrifies me. But I just want to take Stephie home and get us on some kind of schedule." She rolled her eyes. "If that's possible."

Jake nodded thoughtfully. The silence stretched between them. He pondered her situation. It would be easier to offer to stop by her place and check on her now and then. That way, he wouldn't become even more involved with her and the baby than he already was. But Jake Flannery had never been one to take the easy way out. "Well, I suppose I could stay on at your place for a while. To sort of help out when things get rough."

She looked relieved. "You wouldn't mind?"

"Why would I mind?"

"You've already done so much, Jake. I feel uncomfortable asking for more."

His heart softened at the look on her face. She was actually reaching out to him for the first time. She was admitting that she needed someone. Him. Under any other circumstances he would have been thrilled. Okay, so maybe he was still thrilled despite the fact he knew he was heading for heartbreak. He took her hand. "You aren't asking. I'm offering. There's a difference."

Sammie felt a tear slide down her cheek. "Why are you doing this?"

He was asking himself that same question. He squeezed her hand. It didn't matter that he was acting against his own better judgment. "We've been through this whole pregnancy thing together," he said. "I'm not going to abandon you now when I think you need me most."

Jake arrived at the hospital shortly before ten o'clock the following morning. He found Sammie dressed in the same outfit as the night before, trying to put the wriggling infant in her going-home outfit and laughing self-consciously at her clumsy efforts. "I really haven't gotten the hang of this yet," she confessed.

He chuckled. The baby looked anything but happy. Her fists were balled tightly, and her face was red and scrunched as though she were about to cut loose on a crying binge never before seen. "Don't worry, she can't legally move out until she's eighteen. That should give you time to learn." He glanced around the room. "Everything ready?" he said.

"Yes. The bags are all packed, and my doctor has given me the green light. I just have to tell the nurse. There now, that should do it," she said, slipping the lightweight cotton gown into place. As if acting on cue, the nurse appeared with a wheelchair and insisted Sammie get into it. Stephie was then tucked into her mother's arms, and they were wheeled out of the room and into an elevator with Jake following close behind carrying Sammie's bags. He was acutely aware of the stares they received. Men, women, and children alike stopped to peer at the bundle in Sammie's arms and smile. They glanced at Sammie, then at him, and he was certain they were trying to decide which one of them the baby most resembled. It felt awkward. He was ready for a little privacy.

They'd barely had time to get into the Jeep before Sammie took a deep, shaky breath. "Well, I guess this is it." She sniffed.

Jake started the car and pulled forward, checking his mirrors for approaching traffic. He was glad to be leaving the hospital, the smell of disinfectant and above all, Nurse Ratchet, whom he'd already run into twice since Sammie left the labor area. "Yep, this is it," he said.

Sammie sniffed again.

"Hope you're not getting a cold," Jake said, craning his neck so he could see the small sports car coming around him, then before he knew what was happening, Sammie burst into tears. Jake slammed on the brakes, thinking something had hit them, or that she was in great pain. In the back, Stephie was jolted awake and broke into a piercing howl. Jake didn't know who to help first.

"What is it?" he asked Sammie, searching her face frantically.

"I'm going to make a lousy mother," she wailed. Tears welled up in her eyes. She nodded toward the backseat. "And she knows it."

Jake reached into the backseat, trying to offer comfort to the baby. "What?"

"I don't know the first thing about babies," she said. "Who am I trying to fool?"

He was at a loss as to what to do. All he knew was he had to stop the crying. From both of them. "You know how to hold her and feed her."

More tears. "That's not enough, Jake. I mean, for right now it is, but what happens in the future when she comes to expect more from me and . . . and I can't give it?" She paused and wiped her eyes. "Sure, I can bake cookies and volunteer as room mother, but what do I do when she wants to date at thirteen? You know what it's like out there in the real world. But if I don't let her do these things she'll hate me."

The Jeep stalled. Jake put it into gear and turned off the engine. They were sitting in the middle of the parking lot but at least he wasn't blocking traffic. Maneuvering himself so that he was facing the backseat, he unbuckled the screaming infant and carefully pulled her against him. He'd only held her once, reluctantly, and he didn't feel any more comfortable doing so now, but he had to stop the wailing before his head exploded. Sammie didn't seem capable of doing it at the moment. He patted the baby's bottom.

"Listen to me, Sammie," he said at last. "You've been through tougher challenges than this."

"Oh, Lord, what if I can't care for Stephanie any better than my parents could me? What if she has to go through her entire life feeling she was unloved?" she cried.

"That's not going to happen, and you know it," he said, patting softly when the baby started to calm down.

"But what if something happens to me, and I'm no longer capable of caring for her? What if—?"

"Stop it, Sammie!" he hissed, resisting the urge to shake her. She wasn't making sense. "If something happens to you, heaven forbid, *I'll* take care of her."

She blinked several times. "You would?"

"Of course I would. You don't think I'd let anything happen to your daughter, do you?" She pondered that for a moment. The tears stopped. "Look, you're just going through that postpartum business," he said. "Remember when we talked about that in class, and you said it sounded silly, and you wouldn't go through it? Well, welcome to the baby blues, kiddo."

She sniffed and wiped her eyes. "You really think that's what it is?"

"Hormonal changes. That's *exactly* what it is. I think I need to get both of you home and put you to bed, that's what I think." He glanced down at the baby and saw that she had fallen asleep. Being as careful as he could, he returned her to the car seat and strapped her in. She didn't open her eyes.

Jake turned around in his seat and put a finger to his lips. "Okay," he whispered. "Let's go home."

TEN

The ride to her apartment complex was quick, but Sammie found she could barely keep her eyes open by the time they arrived. She paid scant notice to the yardman working on a nearby flower bed as she trudged up the stairs to her door with Jake following close behind carrying the car seat.

Inside it was cool and smelled of the pot-pourri she kept in various jars and boxes. Sammie was glad she'd given the place a thorough cleaning before she went in the hospital. Jake followed her into her bedroom and set the car seat on her bed.

"What do you want me to do with her?" he asked, once he'd unfastened the baby. She'd begun to fidget the second he'd cut the Jeep's engine. Now she was wide awake and growing unhappier by the minute.

"Just hold tight until I slip into something comfortable," Sammie said. "It's almost time for her feeding." She opened the suitcase and brought out her gown, then disappeared into the bathroom.

Jake gazed at the baby and wondered how anything so little could be so perfectly developed. He resisted the urge to open one tiny fist and study her fingers. No doubt she would howl him into the next room over that. Still, he had never seen smaller feet and toes. He could smell her baby scent.

He wondered what Nathan would have thought of her. He wondered what sort of father Nathan would have made. He decided he didn't want to think about either.

Sammie returned wearing a mint-green knee-length gown just as Stephie was beginning to fuss. It was the first time Jake could remember seeing Sammie in that color, and he wanted to tell her how nice it looked on her. Her hair fell softly against her shoulders, thick and shiny. Her breasts were full and lush and pleasantly feminine. She held her arms out, and he suddenly realized he was staring.

"I'll take her now," she said.

"Get in bed first," he told her, reaching around to pull the covers down. She looked unusually tired. He hoped the doctor hadn't released her too early. As soon as she climbed between the sheets, he handed her the infant.

The jostling motion made Stephie clench her fists tighter, and she looked as though she might cry.

"It's okay, sweet pea," Sammie said, fumbling with her gown.

Jake watched as the baby latched on to a nipple and began to suck heartily. He slid the bassinet closer to the bed. "I'm going to make you a sandwich," he said, deciding to leave them alone for a while. Although Sammie claimed it was perfectly okay for him to be in the room while she nursed the baby, he still sensed her discomfort at times. He didn't know if it was because of him or because she didn't feel confident yet in her new role as mother. "I'll be back in a few minutes."

Jake stepped out of the room and closed the door softly behind him, then went into her neat kitchen and found the fixings for a sandwich. He would get her to make a grocery list later.

Sammie had just finished nursing Stephie when Jake appeared with a turkey and cheese on whole wheat and a glass of milk. She put the sleeping baby in the bassinet and ate the sandwich quickly.

"Did you not get enough sleep last night?" he asked, noting the weariness in her eyes.

"I had a lot on my mind."

"Want to talk about it?"

"You'll think it's silly."

"Try me."

Sammie leaned back against her pillows. "I've decided not to remarry after all."

He was amused that she was doing so much deep thinking these days. "What changed your mind?"

"Stephie. I couldn't stand the thought of marrying a man who wasn't good to her. You hear all these stories about stepfathers. And what man is going to love her as much as her natural father would have?"

Jake really didn't feel comfortable discussing other men with her. Still, he should at least try and reassure her. "I think any man who falls in love with you is just naturally going to fall in love with your daughter," he said, wondering what man wouldn't be smitten with the both of them. "I mean, just look at her." They both peered into the bassinet where the baby was sleeping, her tiny feet tucked close to her body.

"Would I sound prejudiced if I told you I thought she was the most beautiful baby in the world?" Sammie said.

He shook his head. "It's the truth. I compared her to all the babies in the nursery, and she was the prettiest. The other babies had red wrinkled faces and were bald."

"Stephie's kind of bald, though, don't you think?" Sammie asked worriedly.

"Not *bald* bald."

"And her face is red."

"Not like the others. The other babies were

downright ugly, Sammie. There were a couple—" He paused and shuddered. "I would have been ashamed to bring them home if they'd been mine. I don't mean to sound nasty, but just looking at how ugly some of those kids were had me dreading running into the parents."

"I'm glad Stephie's a pretty baby." Sammie sighed happily and closed her eyes.

"Try to rest now," Jake said, unplugging the phone on her night table.

Sammie opened her eyes. "Jake?"

He paused at the door. "Hmmm?"

"Thank you."

When Sammie opened her eyes, she'd been sleeping for some time. She looked at the clock on the nightstand and saw that it was coming up to four o'clock. Lord, she and Stephie had practically slept all day. As if acting on cue, the baby stirred. Sammie smiled, pushed the covers aside, and went to her. She winced, still sore from the delivery. Her breasts felt heavy.

"Hello, beautiful little girl," she said softly, as she looked down in the bassinet. Her daughter's eyes were open. Very gently, Sammie picked her up and held her close. "You're wet, aren't you?" she said. She lay the baby on the bed and reached for her diaper bag. By the time she'd changed her, Stephie was beginning to fuss. Sammie climbed back on the bed and began nursing her.

Jake tapped on the door, opened it, and peeked inside. "I thought I heard you up." He pushed the door open farther and stepped inside the room. He smiled, wondering if she'd heard him pressing his ear to the door several times earlier to see if they had awakened yet. "Did you guys get enough sleep?"

Sammie smiled as well. "Yes, and I'm feeling ten times better."

She looked better. The weariness around her eyes was gone. "Ruby stopped by with dinner, but refused to let me wake you. She said she'd call you later." He grinned. "She wants to know when you're going to let her baby-sit."

Sammie chuckled as she stroked the baby's cheek. "Tell her as soon as I can fit into something other than maternity clothes." With her free hand, she patted the bed. "Come sit." She watched him cross the room to sit on the edge of the bed. "So what have you been doing all this time?"

"I ran by the station for a couple of hours. Caught up on paperwork, chatted with the boys to see what's going on."

"Are you sure you can afford the time off?"

He grinned. "I haven't taken a vacation or a sick day since the mid-eighties. I reckon I've got some time coming to me. Actually, I think the captain is glad to get me out of his hair for a while. He claims I'm responsible for his ulcer."

"I don't expect you to sit here with us every day," Sammie told him.

Jake didn't seem to be listening. He was watching the baby nurse. "She looks like you."

Sammie glanced down at the baby. "You really think so? They say it's hard to tell when they're this young."

"I can tell. She has your coloring too."

"Do you think she looks anything like Nathan?"

He shrugged. "Maybe we'll notice it more when she's a little older."

"His parents were disappointed that I didn't take them up on their invitation. I thought his mother's eyes were going to pop right out of her head when I told her you would be staying with me for a while. Ruby was the only one who didn't seem surprised."

Jake reached over and patted her leg. "You have to do what's right for you," he said. He grinned after a moment. "You allowed to eat popcorn?"

"I don't see why not."

"I rented us a couple of videos while I was out. I figured we could move the bassinet into the living room."

"Videos, huh? I hope you didn't rent anything R-rated," she said, trying to sound stern.

"You know I only allow Stephie to watch G movies."

"Don't tell me you're going to be one of those strict parents."

"Darn right I am. I've decided she can't date until she's twenty-five."

He shook his head. "Poor kid. I can see I'm going to have to work on loosening you up."

Once Sammie finished nursing the baby, Stephie drifted off to sleep again, so she put her in the bassinet. "I feel like having a cup of coffee."

"Decaf, right?"

She wrinkled her nose. "If I must."

"I'll make it," he said. "Come sit at the kitchen table so you can tell me where everything is. You need to stay off your feet."

"My doctor wants me up and around," she insisted as she took a chair at the table.

He shot her a dark look. "It's your first day home, for Pete's sake. Give it time."

Sammie knew it was useless to argue with him so she kept quiet as he measured the coffee. It had never occurred to her that he was so domesticated. Although she'd never seen his place, she imagined him living in a bachelor pad with dirty clothes and beer cans strewn across the floor.

"What's your house like?" she asked.

He paused. "Except for the fact that I should probably buy more furniture, it's pretty nice. I got a good deal on it because it needed so much work."

"Do you have a yard?"

He nodded. "A big one with fruit trees."

"I'd love to have a yard for Stephie to play in when she's older."

"They're nice. Except for when you have to mow the lawn."

"That's why Nathan wanted to live in an apartment," she said. "So he wouldn't have to take care of a yard. I like it myself. When I was growing up I used to volunteer for the yard work. The other girls washed dishes and ironed clothes while I pulled weeds and cut grass." She smiled. "I preferred it that way."

Jake looked thoughtful. "My old man couldn't get me to do a damn thing around the house unless he threatened me with my life. Now, I wish I lived close enough to help. I'm sure it's too much for him."

"How is he, by the way?"

"Hating the diet the doctor put him on. The only reason he stays on it is because my mother is carrying her rolling pin around and swears she'll knock him over the head if he doesn't follow doctor's orders."

"Have they been married a long time?" Sammie asked.

"All their lives just about."

"He must not be a cop," she said, her voice taking on a bitter edge.

The room went silent. The coffee maker gurgled and spit. Jake filled two cups and carried them to the table, then brought over the cream and sugar.

"Not all cops get shot, Sammie," he said. "The odds of it happening are slim."

"Don't tell *me* about odds, Jake. I *know* all about them." He held up his hand as though to surrender. She took a sip of coffee, wishing she hadn't been so abrupt. "You've been shot before?"

He nodded. "In the shoulder. It wasn't serious."

"And you've killed people?" She already knew the answer. He'd killed the man who'd killed Nathan.

His eyes clouded. "Twice," he said. "Both times I had no choice."

"How do you live with it?"

"It's not easy. But when you know it's either them or you. . . ." He saw the hard look in her eyes. "What can I tell you, Sammie?"

"I guess I'm waiting for you to admit it's a dangerous job."

"At times. Just like driving a bus or running a convenience store."

"That's different and you know it."

He was getting irritated with her. "Why are we having this discussion anyway? Why do you care what I do for a living?"

"I care. Take my word for it."

They drank their coffee in silence. Jake was the first to break it. "I've been a cop for a long time, Sammie. You know what it means to me. I like what I do. I like knowing when I go to bed at night that I've managed to get one more piece of scum off the streets for a while." He paused. "If there's danger involved, it's just the price I have to pay."

She drained the rest of her coffee and set her cup down with a thump. "I'll never be willing to pay that price again," she said, rising from her seat. "Excuse me, I have to check on the baby."

Jake sat there for a few more minutes, wondering what was going on with her.

"She's beautiful! Absolutely beautiful." Ruby cuddled the baby in her arms and confessed she'd never seen such a gorgeous little girl. "She's gained weight since I saw her in the hospital," she said. "I'll bet she weighs a good ten pounds."

Sammie smiled proudly. "I take her to the doctor tomorrow. We'll see how much she's gained. She eats all the time. Jake says he's going to have to buy her a T-bone steak if she doesn't slow down."

"How is Jake, by the way?" Ruby asked.

"Same as always. He never changes. I don't know what I'd do without him."

"Sounds like love to me."

"Get serious, Ruby."

"I *am* serious." She gazed at the baby. "He'd make a wonderful father."

"Stop." Sammie thought of the conversation she and Jake had had two days earlier. "Nothing is going to happen between us, Ruby, so stop dreaming."

"You can't blame me for wanting the best for my granddaughter." Ruby had declared Stephie her grandchild the first time she'd laid eyes on her.

"Then you'll have to trust me to provide for her," Sammie said. "Frankly, I think I'm going to make a wonderful mother." She sounded more confident than she felt, but in the past few days she'd grown more comfortable with her daughter.

"Of course you will, dear," Ruby said. "I just worry about you."

"Don't." Sammie took the baby from her. "Now, tell me how the store is doing. Is the groomer working out okay?"

Jake went back to work the following week. The narcotics unit, in cooperation with DEA and custom officials, had been planning for weeks to search a local seafood operation that was reputed to be one of the biggest cocaine dealers in the city. The Seafood Station was located in the heart of the city and run by a large family from New Jersey. Several times a day, delivery trucks from coastal areas delivered fresh fish, shrimp, and oysters. Although the Seafood Station sold food in large quantities to neighboring restaurants and grocery stores, they also had a small store in front open to the public.

Jake obtained a search warrant and they raided the place, but neither his unit nor the DEA found anything. They tore open cardboard boxes of bread crumbs and hush-puppy mix and dug through crates of seafood packed in ice until Jake feared his fingers would freeze and break off completely. They came out smelling of fish, with the owners, Martin and Max Felder, cussing and threatening to sue.

Jake was still in a foul mood when he walked through the front door of Sammie's apartment that evening.

Sammie, in the process of burping the baby, gave him a peck of a kiss on his cheek and wrinkled her nose. "Did you go fishing today?" she asked.

He couldn't stay in a bad mood when he saw her. She looked pretty in baggy walking shorts and a white short-sleeve blouse. Her hair was braided and tied off with a small bow. "Fishing for evidence," he said. He told her about the raid, but was interrupted by a wet burp. "Did you do that?" he asked her.

"No, silly. It was the baby."

He stroked the baby's head. "So which one

of us is cooking dinner tonight?" he said, wanting to put the day behind him.

"I was planning to do it," she told him. "But you might want to change the menu after what you went through today."

"I'm so hungry, I could eat a bear," he said.

She chuckled. "I wasn't planning on bear," she told him. "I was planning on baked trout."

He almost shuddered. "You're kidding, right?"

She became defensive. "How was I supposed to know you were going to raid a seafood restaurant today? When Ruby called and offered to run by the grocery store for me, I told her I was being careful about my weight and wanted something healthy. She went by the Seafood Station—"

"Oh, jeez, she went *there*?" He rolled his eyes and shook his head as he made his way into the kitchen where a large whole trout lay on a piece of freezer paper. "We're going to have to eat him with his head on and his eyes looking at us?" he said in disbelief. "I suppose all of his guts are still inside of him too."

Sammie yanked the fish from him. "He doesn't have his guts, he's hollow. Now, stop playing with our dinner and let's take a walk."

"How can he be hollow, they haven't even cut him open?"

She sighed. "I don't know, Jake, maybe they have some special gadget. Frankly, I don't care."

Sammie picked up the baby and walked toward the door. "Are you coming with us? The fresh air will do you good. Besides, I want to try out the new stroller."

He followed her, grabbing the folded stroller before stepping outside. "Why don't you and Stephie have the trout, and I'll make me a peanut butter sandwich?" he suggested as they made their way down the stairs.

"I'm trying to teach you a few healthy habits while you're here," she said.

"I don't want to be healthy. Not if I have to eat something that's looking at me."

Jake rolled the stroller down the sidewalk a few minutes later, but Stephie frowned and squinted, having a miserable time. She sucked on a fist. "She's not hungry again, is she?" Jake said. "Lord, this kid eats more than her mother."

Sammie slapped his shoulder playfully. "I do not eat that much. Anymore," she added. The day was nice, the late-afternoon sun warm on her face. She linked her arm through Jake's and smiled down at her daughter. "What do you think of your new wheels, sugar plum?" she cooed to the baby who didn't give any indication that she'd heard.

"Sugar plum?" Jake asked. "I thought you'd decided on sweet pea."

She nudged him. The baby whimpered, and Jake stopped pushing. Sammie hurried around to the front. "It's okay, sweetie, Mommy's here.

Don't you like your new stroller? Is Daddy pushing you too fast?" Sammie froze the minute the words left her mouth, and a red-hot blush stained both cheeks. She was too embarrassed to look at Jake. Maybe he hadn't heard her. She glanced up and found him watching her with a look of mild amusement, and she knew he had.

"I'm sorry. I don't know what I was thinking."

"It's okay," he said.

"No, it's not okay. I don't want you to get the wrong idea."

"Like what?"

"Like—" She paused and blushed again. "Like I'm trying to find a father for my child."

He merely stared back at her. "Why would I think that?" he said. "You've never once given me a reason to believe there could be anything between us."

"And you know perfectly well the reasons for that," she quipped. She glanced at her watch. "We'd better head back. It's cooling off. I don't want Stephie to get chilled."

Jake wanted to tell her the only chill in the summer afternoon air was coming from her, but he didn't. Instead, he turned the stroller around and headed for home. They said very little on the way back. At the bottom of the stairs, Sammie plucked the baby out of the canvas seat and carried her upstairs. Jake folded the stroller and followed her inside. He stood there for a moment, not knowing what to say or do. Finally, he walked to the door of Sammie's bedroom.

Sammie, having tucked the baby beneath a receiving blanket in her bassinet, turned. She stiffened when she saw him standing there, watching her with a strange look on his face. "What?"

"Are you going to avoid me now?" he asked.

"I wasn't avoiding you."

He stepped closer. "Talk to me, Sammie. We've been through too much to let something come between us." When she didn't answer, he walked over to her. He raised his hand to her cheek and stroked it. "You've always been able to say exactly what you were thinking to me. What's changed?"

He was standing so close, she could feel the heat from his body. She wanted to tell him how she was feeling, *longed* to tell him, but she didn't dare. Her eyes teared. She shook her head. Darn but she was crying a lot these days. She swiped the tears, embarrassed. "It must be my hormones again," she said. "Making me feel things—"

He turned his hand inward, cupping her face with his palm as he gazed into her eyes. "What kinds of things, babe?"

She wished he wouldn't turn tender on her. Anything but that. It had been so long. "Jake, I have to level with you," she began, trying to choose her words carefully. "I've always tried to be straightforward—" He locked his black eyes with hers, impaled her. She almost shivered.

"What?"

She took a deep, shuddering breath. "I care for you. More than I should. Not just as a friend anymore."

He looked surprised, then thoughtful. He stepped closer, within an inch of her. "So what are we going to do about it?"

She lowered her gaze to his chest and when she spoke her voice was a mere whisper. "I don't know."

Jake crooked one finger and nudged her chin so that she was forced to look into his eyes once more. "Know what I think?" When she didn't answer, he went on. "I think we should make the best of it."

ELEVEN

Sammie barely had time to register the words before his lips descended, and she was in no way prepared for the kiss. Jake had kissed her many times during the past months, on the forehead and cheek, a couple of brief pecks on the lips, but nothing like this. She knew she was in trouble the minute his mouth opened over hers.

The sensation—his skin touching hers—was jolting and mind-boggling, everything she had imagined it would be. As he prodded her lips apart with his tongue, he pulled her closer, enveloping her in his scent and the feel of his body. She leaned into the embrace, wanting, no, *needing* to be held for once.

The kiss deepened as he explored her mouth with his tongue. Sammie felt a rush of heat inside. At the same time, her thoughts turned chaotic. What was she doing, kissing this man back?

It served no purpose other than to draw her closer to him. That was the last thing she needed.

Without letting her go, Jake walked her to the bed. She felt the mattress at the back of her knees, felt him lower her. She tried to pull away, but he held her in a firm grip.

He lay down beside her, wedging one knee between her thighs, pushing against her so she had no doubt of his arousal. The heat spread throughout her body. He slipped one hand beneath her blouse and cupped her breast. She could feel the warmth of his hand through her bra. Her breasts swelled in response. They ached. She twisted her mouth free.

"Jake, I can't," she whispered as his touch became even more bold. "It's too early."

"What?"

"It's too soon after the baby," she said.

Jake snatched his hand from beneath her blouse and bolted upright. He raked both hands through his hair. "Damn, I wasn't thinking. I'm sorry."

"It's not your fault," she said, blushing self-consciously. "I was beginning to—" She paused. "You know."

Jake studied her for a moment. "I thought Sally said new mothers weren't easily aroused."

She smiled shyly. "Maybe Sally doesn't know everything." Still, she knew part of the reason she'd gone as far as she had was simply the need to be held. The other—that brief spurt of desire —had come as a surprise.

"So when can you?" Jake said. "I don't think we covered that subject in class."

"Not for several more weeks." He looked disappointed. "I don't think that's something either of us should anticipate," she said. "After all, we have serious differences."

He knew precisely what she was talking about. "Really? We only have one difference that I'm aware of."

"One *big* difference."

"So you're telling me I have a choice. If I want to pursue this, I give up the job I love. Otherwise, I back off." She looked away without answering. Jake shrugged, climbed off the bed and headed for the door. "Looks like I stand to lose either way." He left the room before she could respond.

"Are you going to stay angry with me forever?" Sammie asked Jake the following evening. She had just cleaned up the dinner dishes and put the baby to bed when she went looking for him. She found him sitting on the front steps.

Jake glanced up at the sound of her voice. He'd been lost in his own thoughts. "What?"

"I said if you're going to stay mad at me you might as well go home."

"Sit down, Sammie." He indicated the step

next to him. When she didn't move, he frowned. "Okay, please."

She sat down. The steps barely accommodated the two of them. Thighs and shoulders were pressed flush. He didn't say anything. She waited.

"How do you expect me to feel?" he asked at last, regarding her with a slight tilt to his head. "I've done everything in my power to support you these past eight months. To be there for you. I suspected I was beginning to care for you more than I should, but I wouldn't admit it, even to myself. I'm not some dimwit. I know what you went through after Nathan was shot. I went through some of it too, dammit!"

"What are you trying to say, Jake?"

"You shouldn't have told me you cared about me unless you were willing to do something about it."

This made her angry. "I had a weak moment. So sue me." She paused. "I wish I hadn't said anything."

"But you do love me, right? Just as I love you."

He'd said he loved her.

"Answer me."

"Yes!"

"Say it."

"I love you! Why are you doing this?"

"Because I love you more than I've ever loved another human being, and I want you to know damn good and well what you're giving up 'cause of your unreasonable attitude."

She glared at him. "Go to hell, Jake." She started to get up, but he stopped her.

"You're scared to death, aren't you, Sammie?"

The tears came. "So, maybe I am. Can you blame me? What am I supposed to do, Jake, sit around and watch the same thing happen to you that happened to Nathan? Pace the floor every night until you come home, scared out of my wits because you might be dead?"

"A lot of policemen's wives have experienced those feelings from time to time. They've learned to deal with it."

"Well, bully for them. Just wait until they have to bury the man they love. I guarantee they won't be standing in line to do it a second time."

Jake saw that he was getting nowhere, and he was genuinely angry. "I had no idea your and Nathan's marriage was so wonderful," he said, sarcasm slipping into his voice.

She snapped her head around, studying him intently. "What's that supposed to mean?"

"Nathan and I went by the Pit one night. He drank too much as he was inclined to do once in a while. He told me you two were seriously thinking of splitting up, said the marriage had problems from the beginning and that you'd only married him because you wanted a baby so badly."

Her cheeks flamed. "You knew that all along and never said anything?"

"He also told me, the morning of the shooting, that you had spoken with a lawyer. Makes me wonder if maybe you haven't been feeling more guilty than grief-stricken over his death."

"You bastard! You'll stop at nothing to get what you want," she said. "Is that how you get answers back at the station, Jake? By going straight for the jugular? I thought you were my friend."

His eyes could have penetrated concrete as he fixed her with a heated stare. "I don't want to be your friend anymore, Sammie. I want more. I want Stephie to—"

"What about Stephie?" she said, tossing her head back. "You want her to think of you as her daddy? So that she can worry herself sick every time you leave the house? Is that what you want?" She wiped her eyes and sniffed. "As for Nathan, I *was* going to file for a divorce. Then I discovered I was pregnant. I decided that might be the miracle we needed to make the marriage work. Unfortunately, he never came home that night. He never knew he was going to be a father."

Jake stood up. The anger was gone, replaced with a weariness. "So where do we go from here, Sammie?"

She glanced away. "We go back to how it was

before. Friends. Nothing more, nothing less. Besides, it was good between us, Jake."

His eyes grew sad, yet resigned. "Not as good as it could have been, babe."

Jake left for work earlier than usual the next morning, hoping to avoid running into Sammie. He'd heard the baby cry as he was coming out of his room, heard Sammie speak to her, but she hadn't ventured out and he decided she was about as eager to face him as he was her. He regretted now that he'd told her he'd known about her crumbling marriage. How like him to just spout off at the mouth without thinking. What was wrong with him anyway? He was in love, that's what it was. They said men did foolish things in that condition, well, he'd proved that saying right.

As soon as he got to the station, Jake knocked on the captain's door. "I need another search warrant," he told the man. "I want to take a second look at that seafood operation."

Captain Mitchell took a swig of his antacid and wiped his mouth. "Forget it. The brass raked me over the coals for the mess your men made searching that place. The owners have already talked to their lawyer. This is not a good time to go back."

"I know they're dealing, Captain."

"Yeah, well, knowing and proving are two

different things. These guys got their hands in more than seafood here. You know those parking lots all over town? Who do you think owns most of them? I figure those parking lots will pay for one helluva good lawyer."

"They're stuffing the coke in the body cavity of the trout they sell," Jake said as though he hadn't heard a word.

The captain looked impatient now. "Do you know that for a fact, Flannery? Are you one hundred percent positive? Can you walk into that place and put your hands right on it?"

Jake hesitated. He'd lain awake half the night thinking about it. It was the only way. "I'm fairly sure."

"Not good enough. Look, you got plenty of other cases. Concentrate on them for a while. We can always come back to these guys."

"They'd have time to clear out by then," Jake told him. "They won't expect us to come back this soon."

The other man glared at him. "I believe I've already answered your question, Flannery, and the answer was no. I'm still in charge here last I heard, and that's all I've got to say on the subject."

"We're gonna get in big trouble over this," one of Jake's men said, as they pulled their van in front of the Seafood Station.

"No, we're not," Jake assured him. "We're not searching the place. We just came to buy something. There's a big difference."

"We're still gonna get in trouble," the man repeated. "The captain is gonna chew our butts to ribbons."

"Not when we bust this place wide open. He'll be pinning medals on us." Jake chuckled as he said it. Everybody knew Captain Mitchell had it in for Jake Flannery. Some said it was because the other man feared Jake would snatch his job away one day. Jake didn't want the job any more than the captain wanted to relinquish it. Jake preferred the action on the streets to kissing a bunch of politicians' butts. One of these days he might share his feelings with Mitchell, but for now he enjoyed antagonizing him.

They climbed out of the van. "Just let me do all the talking," Jake said as they paused outside the front door of the store.

"What the hell are you guys doing back here?" Max Felder, one of the owners of the Seafood Station demanded when they walked through the door. "Didn't you cause enough trouble last time? We still haven't cleaned up that mess. Don't think you won't be hearing from our lawyer. My brother's over there talking to him right now."

Jake was glad to hear the other brother wasn't on the premises. He was certain Martin Felder wouldn't have a problem pulling a gun on them. "We came to buy seafood," Jake said, spreading his hands innocently. "Nothing wrong with that, is there?" Max didn't answer him. He just glared. Jake shrugged and leaned against the long white case that held a variety of seafood on ice. "What looks good, boys?" he said.

"Shrimp looks nice," one of them said.

"Hey, get a load of that trout," Jake said. "I just had some last night, and it was great." The owner continued to glare. Jake was certain the man knew he was lying. "Just one question, Max. How come you leave the heads on?"

"Are you going to buy something or are you going to stand there all day wasting my time?" the man said.

"I'll take all you got."

Max looked bored. "All of what?"

"Your trout."

This got his attention. His head snapped up. "What do you mean, *all* of them?" he said in a voice that suggested Jake must be crazy. "I got a couple of hundred pounds of this stuff."

"Good. That's about how much we're going to need, aren't we, boys? And just to make sure there's none left lying around, I'm going to personally assist you in bringing it out of the cooler in back."

The man's face became red. "What do you think you're doing?" he demanded. "You have no use for that much fish."

"We're going to have a dinner party, aren't

we, guys?" The others nodded. "By the way, Max, what kind of wine would you recommend we serve with this?"

The owner looked flustered. He glanced around quickly as though looking for someone to bail him out of his predicament. "I can't sell you my entire stock," he said. "We've already promised some of it to other customers."

Jake reached inside his jacket and unsnapped the holster holding his gun. He knew he didn't have any legal right to draw it on the man so he'd have to bluff his way through it. "Tell you what," he said. "We can either do this my way or you can resist and face the consequences." It wasn't a threat. Not at all.

Sweat beaded on Max's forehead and upper lip as he eyed the gun and the big men who were waiting. "I'd like to try and reach my brother first."

"No time, Max. We're in a bit of a hurry."

Finally, the other man looked resigned. "The cooler is this way," he said.

Sammie learned about the bust on the six o'clock news. She was nursing Stephie and waiting for Jake to come home when the Channel Five anchorwoman announced a drug bust at a local business. They showed footage of narcotics officers pulling fish out of a cooler, trout stuffed with cocaine. All at once, a microphone was thrust in Jake's face.

"The owner of the Seafood Station claims it was an illegal search and seizure," the newswoman said.

Jake looked surprised. "We weren't searching the place," he said. "We were buying fish for a dinner party. I was just surprised to see that some of the trout was stuffed and some wasn't. You can imagine how shocked I was to discover drugs inside. By the way, do you know what color wine goes best with fish?"

Sammie chuckled as she watched. "You're full of it, Jake Flannery." She glanced up when the front door opened and he stepped inside. "Speak of the devil," she muttered.

Jake closed the door behind him. "How are my girls?" he asked. He kissed Sammie on the forehead and tickled Stephie's bare feet. The baby stopped sucking for a second, then proceeded with a gusto that made them laugh.

"You're famous," Sammie told him, pointing to the TV screen, just as it flashed to a commercial.

He grinned, thankful for the diversion so they didn't have to talk about their argument the night before. "Yeah, I reckon I'll have to get an agent now and all that."

"So when's the dinner party? Should I buy a new outfit?"

He continued to smile. "If you saw what that

trout looked like when we finished digging through it." He shook his head sadly. "The police van is probably ruined from the smell."

"Oh, well, you're a hero, so what does one van matter?"

"Not exactly," Jake said. "The captain wasn't speaking to me this afternoon. I have a feeling he's about to come down hard on me."

"Why?"

"He asked me to lay off this case for a while because he's afraid the owners are going to sue. They've got money and connections. Not your average dealers. Their records are squeaky clean."

"How'd you find out about them?"

"I've got contacts on the street. People who want to beat a rap. Folks will rat on their own mother to keep from going to prison."

"What a nice thought," she said, sarcasm slipping into her voice. "You must look forward to working with those kind of people day in and day out."

He frowned. So they were back to that. "Don't start on me, Sammie. What I need right now is a cold beer not a lecture." He made his way toward the kitchen. "How about I cook tonight?" he said, opening the refrigerator.

Sammie finished nursing Stephie and pulled her blouse into place. She carried the baby into the kitchen. "How about I take you out to dinner instead?" she said, irritated with herself for bringing up his job again. After their argument the night before, she had decided to try and stick to safe topics. So why did she insist on blurting things out without thinking?

He pulled out his beer and closed the refrigerator. "Say what?"

"Ruby offered to baby-sit so I could get out for a while. Frankly, I need it. I thought if you didn't have plans we could go to the mall. I need to pick up a few baby things."

"Ruby's going to baby-sit?" he asked. "What about the other thing?" At her blank look, he went on. "You know, the breast-feeding part?"

"I've taken care of that with my breast pump."

Now it was his turn to look confused. A breast pump? He imagined her using some heavy metal object like the pumps folks used to get water out of their basements. Damned if women didn't have more gizmos and gadgets to carry around in their purses. All a man needed was a change of clothes and his car keys. "I don't have the slightest idea what you're talking about," he said. "I'll just have to take your word for it. As for *you* taking *me* out—"

"I insist, Jake," she interrupted. "It's the least I can do after all you've done for me."

He stepped closer, leaned down and touched the baby's head with his lips although he would have preferred kissing Sammie. He raised up and looked into her beautiful eyes. He'd noticed them the first time he'd met her, when he'd had absolutely no right noticing. "What have I done for you?"

She wished he wouldn't look at her like that. It made her realize how foolish she'd been to think they could be friends when there was so much more beneath the surface just waiting to be unleashed. She felt it deep in her stomach. "You've always been there for me," she said, as though it should be obvious.

"And now you think you owe me?"

"It's not a matter of owing you. It's a matter of one good turn deserving another. Don't make a big deal out of it, okay? It's only dinner."

The mall was busy with after-work shoppers and teenagers who seemed to be just hanging out. Sammie paused at a pay phone once they walked through the entrance. "Do you think I should call Ruby?"

He gave her a funny look. "We just left the house. Why don't you give it another ten minutes."

"You're right. She'll think I don't trust her." Sammie spied a specialty shop offering a twenty-percent discount on baby items and forgot her anxiety for the moment. "Let's start there," she said, taking Jake's hand and leading him inside. She spent the next hour combing through outfits, oohing and aahing over each one and seeing that Jake did the same. Although he would have much preferred going into the electronics store next door, he made himself stay. Nevertheless, he was thankful when she finally selected three sleepers and a lightweight jumper.

Jake saw the tiny dress hanging at the front of a rack, beckoning to him. He went for it. "I want to get Stephie this," he said, holding up the pink dress with rosebuds embroidered on the collar.

"Oh, how adorable," Sammie said, fingering the dainty collar. "But you shouldn't, Jake. You already got her flowers and a teddy bear. You'll spoil her."

"She's too young to know she's being spoiled," he told her. "I'll stop buying her things when she's two years old, how's that?"

By the time they approached the counter, Jake had selected a doll, a fire engine, and police car as well.

"What's all this?" Sammie asked, her look disapproving.

"She doesn't have any toys," he pointed out.

"She's too young for toys."

"Kids grow up fast, Sammie. You'll turn around one day and, wham, she's ready for toys, and we won't have a single thing for her. She'll say bad things about us in therapy."

Sammie chuckled. "You're hopeless, you know that?" They paid for the items. "I should probably call now, huh?" she said, as soon as they left the store. She called and found out

Stephie was alive and well and hadn't yet taken her bottle. "We still have time for more shopping," she said. "But first, how about I buy you a hot dog?"

He looked amused. "Is that your idea of taking me out to dinner?"

"I figured you wouldn't want to waste time eating when you could be shopping," she said.

"Oh, that's what you thought." He glanced around. "Well, you're probably right. I noticed there's a sale in that linen outlet store. I'd never forgive myself if I missed it."

She knew he was teasing her, but it felt so good to be out for a change that it didn't matter. She grinned, grabbed his hand and led him to the small hole-in-the-wall restaurant that sold hot dogs, hamburgers, and cheese fries.

"You don't think I'm a bad mother, do you?" Sammie asked, once they'd carried their trays to a table. Each of them had ordered chili dogs and fries smothered in cheese. It wasn't on Sammie's new healthy eating plan, but she figured she deserved a break after being so good.

Jake frowned. "Why would you ask me that?"

"Because, my daughter's not even two weeks old and I'm out shopping and having the time of my life. I really don't even miss her that much to tell you the truth."

"Oh, for heaven's sake, Sammie." He shook his head. As long as he lived he would never understand women. First they moaned because they had to get out, then, the minute you took them somewhere they started feeling guilty about it. "I think it's great you're out," he told her.

"That's what Ruby said when she called to suggest it."

"Ruby talked you into going out?"

She nodded. "She said the baby blues were worse on new mothers if they didn't get out of the house or take time for themselves."

"Well, Ruby should know," he told her. "She's already been through all of this."

"Do you think I should call?"

"What, again? What could possibly have happened in the last twelve minutes?"

"You're right. I don't know what I'm thinking." She ate her hot dog, telling herself she would not think or talk about the baby for the rest of the evening. "You know what I'd like to do?" she said as soon as they finished.

"Shop some more?" he asked.

She chuckled. "No, not shop. I'd like to go to that park down the street. The one with the jogging trail."

"You're not planning on jogging?"

"No, but I'd like to walk."

He was relieved he wasn't going to have to go in another store. "That sounds good to me."

Once they finished dinner, Jake loaded their trash onto one of the trays and dumped it in a garbage can, then grabbed their bags and ushered Sammie out of the restaurant and through the double doors that marked the mall's exit. The early-evening air was pleasant on their faces as they climbed out of Jake's Jeep and crossed the playground area to the jogging trail.

"Now, don't get carried away," he told her as they started to walk at a fast pace.

"I used to run three miles a day until a couple of years ago," Sammie said, tilting her head back and sucking in the fresh air.

"Why'd you give it up?"

She shrugged. "I don't know. I just lost interest, I guess. I stopped sewing and reading and all that good stuff. Just concentrated on the store. One week alone I spent almost one hundred hours there."

Jake wondered if she'd done it to avoid being with Nathan, but he didn't dare ask. It was none of his business, and besides, he didn't want to do or say anything to make her uncomfortable. He could see the tension in her body; she was coiled as tightly as he was. When had they begun to feel uneasy with each other? What had happened to that feeling of camaraderie they'd shared all these months?

He knew perfectly well what was wrong.

They had fallen in love.

They circled the track three times, making nonessential conversation. Finally, Jake suggested they sit the next round out. They found a bench beneath a tree and sat down.

The silence stretched between them.

"Sammie?"

She jumped at the sound of his voice, then laughed self-consciously. Lord, but she was tense. "Yes?"

"This didn't happen overnight for me."

She glanced away. "Please don't say anything, Jake."

He sighed heavily. He couldn't just ignore it, pretend it didn't exist. "I used to look for excuses not to come by your apartment when Nathan invited me."

"Why?"

"Because I didn't want to have to see you or the unhappiness in your eyes." He looked at her. "You don't hide your feelings as well as you think you do. I knew you were miserable. I didn't think Nathan deserved you. I knew if you belonged to me I would do everything in my power to make you happy." He shook his head. "And then—" He paused. "Nathan got killed, and I figured I'd caused it by wishing you were mine."

Sammie's eyes misted. "Like I've said before, I never blamed you for Nathan's death. Nathan chose to be a cop. We both know why it was so important for him to succeed."

"I know I've asked this before, Sammie. What are we going to do? I can't help feeling the way I do about you and the baby."

She didn't answer right away. Instead, she gazed at him for a moment, taking in the handsome face she'd come to love so dearly. "I don't know any other way to say it, Jake. I think you should leave tomorrow."

TWELVE

At first, he didn't want to believe it. She was kicking him out. He had known all along his staying with her was temporary, but he hadn't figured on it coming to an end so quickly. He'd grown accustomed to seeing her at the end of the workday. He looked forward to their good-natured banter, the fact that he could tell her almost anything about himself. He enjoyed watching her bathe Stephie or nurse her till the baby fell asleep at her breast. He enjoyed the simple things, playing cards at the kitchen table, deciding which video to rent for the evening, arguing about whose turn it was to clean the kitchen. Nothing had prepared him for the sheer desolation of not being able to share those things. He was no longer the tough cop, man of steel. He was a human being who'd just had his guts ripped out.

"I see," he said in a voice that belied the emotional turmoil he was feeling. Who would take care of them, see that Sammie didn't overdo it as she was inclined to do?

"We need time away from each other, Jake," she said, noting the hurt in his eyes and hating that it had come to this. But what else could she do? "We've practically been attached at the hip since Nathan died. I need time with my new baby. I need time to think about what's been going on with us."

He didn't respond for several moments. A breeze fluttered the leaves above them. Across the park two boys threw a Frisbee back and forth. "I shouldn't have pushed you," he said. "I should have pretended we were nothing but friends, just as I did in the beginning."

"I'm as much to blame as you are," she said. "Which is why I have to clear my head and figure out what I'm going to do with my life."

With *her* life, he thought, noting she'd excluded him. She hadn't said anything about *their* life or what *they* would do. "You're shutting me out, Sammie. It's like I'm supposed to be able to turn off my feelings"—he snapped his fingers— "just like that. And if I can't, you don't want me around anymore."

"Jake, you knew how I felt about your job from the beginning. This shouldn't come as a surprise."

"Is this why you decided to take me to dinner?" he said, his anger getting the best of him. "So you could tell me to get lost?"

"I'm not telling you to get lost. I'm telling you I need a little space in my life right now. I can't think when you're around."

"Then I'll make it easy for you," he said, reaching into his pocket for the keys to his Jeep. He tossed them to her. "Have a nice evening," he cut her off when she tried to object. He stood and strode away, leaving her on the park bench looking as though she'd lost her best friend.

Which, in fact, she had.

Jake awoke the next morning with a hangover and the need to beat up somebody. He gazed at his bloodshot eyes in the bathroom mirror and told himself how dumb it was to go out and get drunk at his age. By the time he walked into the narcotics unit, having taken a cab to the station, his mood had worsened.

"Hey, something smells fishy," someone said as Jake passed.

Jake ignored the comment, knowing the men would tease him for days over busting the Seafood Station. That was the least of his problems.

"Flannery, get your butt in my office," Captain Mitchell bellowed, causing Jake to wince in pain from his pounding head.

He stepped inside gingerly. "Yeah, what is it?"

The captain frowned when he saw him. "What the hell happened to you?"

"I have a hangover."

"And you expect me to put you on the streets protecting our good citizens?"

"I'm okay." It had taken six aspirin and two glasses of tomato juice, but now he thought he might live.

The captain reached for his antacid bottle, took a swig, and set it down. "You disobeyed my orders regarding that seafood place. Not only that, you performed a major bust without notifying DEA and custom officials, who I might add had every right to be there."

Jake was in no mood for a chewing out. "So I broke a few rules. We got 'em, didn't we?"

"I'm sick and tired of you calling your own shots, Flannery. You're not on your own here, we're part of a team. Anytime you mess something up, the department has to answer for it. Do you have any idea how many people have filed lawsuits against the Atlanta Police Department since you were assigned to the narcotics unit?"

Jake felt too rotten to try and defend himself. "Sometimes we get a little carried away in the heat of the moment," he managed. "Our lives are on the line, what can I say?"

"You made a fool out of this department on TV yesterday, talking about your damn dinner party."

"It was just a joke, Captain."

"A very bad joke, Flannery."

"Okay, so I wouldn't make a great comedian. I'll remember that."

"You're not a great detective at the moment either, Flannery." He scribbled something on a piece of paper and handed it to him. "I'm reassigning you for the time being."

"What?" Jake reached for the slip and read it quickly. "You can't pull me off narcotics while I'm in the middle of several cases."

The captain leaned back in his chair and clasped his hands together behind his head. "I just did. You're on the front desk until otherwise notified."

When Jake got off work, he took a cab straight to Sammie's apartment. He was in such a bad mood, he almost hoped she wasn't home. He got his wish. Her car wasn't in the parking lot. His Jeep was there with the keys under the floor mat. He drove home, swallowed three aspirin, and called her. No answer.

By the end of the week, Jake was beginning to worry. Sitting at the front desk all day, he had plenty of opportunity to call, and she hadn't picked up the phone once. He visited the Curly Q Pet and Grooming Salon during lunch. Ruby paled when she saw him.

"Where is she?" he demanded.

"What do you mean, where is she?" the

older woman asked, as though she didn't have the slightest idea what he was talking about.

"Don't jerk me around, Ruby. I've driven by her place a half-dozen times this week. Where'd she go?"

Ruby sighed and patted her white head. Her hands were trembling. "I can't tell you, Jake. She made me promise. All I can say is, she and the baby are safe and with people who love them."

Jake slammed his fist on the counter so hard, she jumped. Finally, he turned and stalked toward the door. "To hell with her!" he said before stomping out.

Amanda Webster smiled down at Stephie as she changed her wet diaper. "How'd I do?"

Sammie nodded. "I'm impressed. How long did you say it's been?"

The woman groaned and rolled her eyes. "Let's not count. I'll feel like an old woman." She pulled the baby close. "Oh, I'd forgotten how sweet they smell."

Sammie laughed. "Your memory really is bad, Amanda. They don't always smell that sweet."

The older woman laughed as well. "You won't convince me that this little girl ever smells bad." She laid the baby on the bed and played with her toes. Stephie pulled her feet up and made a cooing sound. Her tiny bow mouth twitched. "Look, she smiled at me," Amanda said. "She knows who her grandma is, don't you, sweetie?"

"You know you're spoiling her," Sammie said, trying to sound sternly disapproving.

"So I am. I can't tell you what these past few weeks have meant to me," Amanda said, her eyes tearing. "I've been so low since Nathan died. And embarrassed."

"Embarrassed?"

"For not being there for you in the beginning. Here you were, newly widowed and pregnant, and I was so caught up in my own grief, I couldn't help you. All I can say is thank God for Nathan's friend, Jake."

Sammie nodded. "Yes, he was a big help to me."

Amanda was quiet for a moment. "I thought for sure something would come of it. The relationship, I mean." She searched Sammie's face as she said it. "At first I was hurt that you could care for another man after my son. Then I realized it was only right for you to love again. After all, you had a baby to think of."

"Nothing's going to happen between Jake and me," Sammie said, a sense of desolation washing over her as she spoke the words. "I wouldn't marry another policeman."

"You're in love with him, though, aren't you?"

Sammie nodded, and felt as though she was

about to cry. "Very much. I wouldn't have made it these past months without him."

Amanda looked thoughtful. "You know, Sammie," she began softly. "As much as I suffered over Nathan's death, I would not have given up the experience of knowing him for anything. As painful as it was and still is, I would have preferred knowing him and suffering to never having known him at all." She leaned over and kissed the baby. "And I have a beautiful little granddaughter to remember him by. No matter what happens, Sammie, please don't ever forget I'm Stephie's grandmother."

Sammie took the woman's hand. "Never."

The apartment smelled musty as Sammie stepped through the front door, holding Stephie. Although Ruby had checked her mail and watered her plants, she hadn't wanted to open a window in case it rained.

Sammie carried the baby into her room and strapped her into a new infant seat, then placed it on the kitchen table while she went through her mail. Bills. She had to think about going back to work, despite the money the Websters had given her from Nathan's insurance policy. She wanted to save that money. Not only that, she wanted to get back to doing the things she liked. Besides, it wasn't like she couldn't take Stephie with her.

She owned the place, she could do what she liked.

She put the mail aside and gazed at the baby who seemed fascinated with the ceiling light fixture. It was quiet, oddly quiet after having spent the past three weeks with Nathan's family. She was glad she'd taken them up on their invitation, even though it had been uncomfortable in the beginning. The baby had made the difference, drawing Amanda out of her shell and making her forget her grief for a time.

All the while, Sammie had been missing Jake. Jake, who'd shown her it was okay to need someone once in a while. It didn't seem right sharing her happiness with Nathan's family when Jake was the one who'd supported her through the bad times.

She had never been so lonely in her life. And now, sitting in the quiet apartment, she realized things would never be the same without him.

THIRTEEN

It was late when Jake drove by Sammie's apartment and noted the lights burning inside. He squealed into the parking lot and pulled into a slot in front of her building. He parked, climbed out of the car, and hurried up the stairs. Thinking the baby might be asleep, he knocked softly. Sammie opened the door a moment later, wearing her bathrobe. A towel covered her hair. She'd obviously just stepped from the shower.

She looked surprised to see him. "What are you doing here?"

He didn't know which emotion was stronger, anger or relief. He pushed through the door and closed it behind him. "Where the hell have you been?"

She had never seen him so furious. His eyes looked like a black cloud ready to burst, his lips a grim line. "I spent a few weeks with Nathan's family. At their place on the lake."

"And you didn't even bother to tell me?" he said, his voice accusing. "That stinks, Sammie."

"Ruby—"

"Ruby didn't tell me a damn thing."

"I thought it best, Jake."

"Best for whom? Surely not me. I had to lie awake at night and wonder if you and the baby were okay." He grabbed her by the shoulders. "Sometimes I just want to shake you till—" He paused and gazed down at her. "You just don't get it, do you?" he said, his expression growing weary. "You don't care that I love you, and you don't care if you rip my guts out."

Her eyes misted. "I *do* care, Jake," she said, her voice trembling. "Very much."

It was hard to be angry with her when she looked so sad, so vulnerable. Jake felt himself weakening, felt his insides turn to mush. He tightened his grip on her. "Dammit, Sammie! Why do I let you do this to me?"

She opened her mouth to answer, but he muffled her words by capturing her lips with his. The kiss was hard, almost brutal. She thought she detected cigarette smoke on him. Jake raised his hands to her face and held her still. He didn't realize how rough he was being until he felt her tears on his fingers.

He released her and stepped away, then raked his hands through his hair. "I'm sorry. I don't know what got into me." He took a deep, shuddering breath. "I'm all screwed up right now. I'm sorry," he repeated and turned for the door.

"Don't leave," she said softly.

"I can't take it anymore, Sammie. I can't pretend we're friends when I know there's more to it. I can't look at you without wanting to make love to you."

"I can't go on like this either," she said. At his confused look, she unwound the towel from her head, dropped it on the floor, and combed her hair from her face with trembling fingers. She hesitated only a moment before reaching for the belt on her robe. (Pregnancy and motherhood had left her self-conscious.) She untied it, opened the robe, and let it slide off her shoulders.

Jake's gaze followed. He sighed. "Oh, man." His eyes greedily devoured her—the gentle sloping shoulders, the full pink-tipped breasts. "Oh, man," he repeated. Her waist was slimmer than he would have expected with a five-week-old infant, her hips generous but well proportioned. "What does this mean, Sammie?" he said, raising his eyes to her. "Are you okay? Did the doctor say it was okay?"

"I don't go till the end of the week, but I'm okay." She took his hand and led him into the bedroom.

"Where's Stephie?" he said, when he noticed the empty bassinet.

"In her crib." She smiled. "You didn't come here to play with *her*, did you?" She pretended to be hurt.

He grinned. "No. I came to play with her mother."

He watched her pull the covers down on the bed. "Are you sure you're okay?" He didn't want to rush her. As excited as he was, he was willing to wait if her body wasn't ready.

"Sure I'm sure." She knew she sounded more confident than she felt as she reached for the buttons of his shirt. "I've missed you, Jake," she said softly, then stood on tiptoe to kiss him. Once again, she thought she detected cigarette smoke. She broke the kiss.

"Have you been smoking?"

He looked embarrassed. "Yeah. Is it offensive?"

She chuckled. "Just surprising, that's all." She raised her mouth to his once more.

He ducked so she could reach him, then parted his lips when her shy tongue pressed against them. He took her tongue inside and made love to it, sucking it gently, swirling his own tongue around the tip. He drew her tight against him, fitting her softness against his lean body.

Sammie shivered as his fingers moved along her spine, then dropped to her hips and began kneading them softly. She leaned against him, loving the feel of his wide chest, his hard thighs. She could feel his erection and knew he was holding back, taking his time with her, using great care. She appreciated it. At the same time, she was eager for his lovemaking.

Before long, the kisses grew hot and frantic. Jake sank his tongue deep inside her mouth and explored thoroughly. His hands did the same over her body. He broke the kiss and moved his lips to her throat, her ears and dipped his tongue inside one. Sammie shivered once more.

They moved to the bed. Sammie climbed beneath the covers and waited while Jake undressed. She watched, not the least bit shy about looking at him. She smiled at what she saw. There wasn't an ounce of fat on his body, only brown skin and hard sinew, lightly feathered with the same black hair that topped his head.

She held her arms out to him.

He couldn't get to her fast enough.

Jake had cautioned himself against hurrying, not only because he was afraid of hurting her but because he wanted her to savor their lovemaking. But he only had to look at her to want her. There was something decidedly sexy about making love to a new mother. Those heavy breasts tempted him. He had watched her nurse an infant and now he wanted to taste her for himself. He raised his hands and covered them. Her skin was fair against his dark coloring, smooth against his roughened palm. Finally, when he couldn't put it off any longer, he lowered his head and took one nipple into his mouth. He kissed and suckled and tugged it gently between his lips, then smiled when he tasted her milk.

She slipped her fingers through his black hair as he paid homage to each breast, holding him close, stroking his head as a wave of tenderness washed over her. She wondered at it. Then, all at once, the feelings changed and were replaced with something altogether different, something intense and erotic that warmed her lower belly and made her anxious.

"Touch me, Sammie," he said, grasping her hand in his and moving it to the juncture of his thighs. She closed her palm around him. He sighed. How many times had he dreamed of her doing just that? Even late in her pregnancy when he shouldn't have been thinking such things. Now his blood roared in his ears as she stroked his hardness. He stilled her hand, knowing he needed to take it slow.

He moved his lips to the other breast and spent as much time there as he had the first. Sammie squirmed. Finally, he kissed his way to her navel. He tongued it. Her stomach was still slightly rounded. She was like ripe fruit. He inched past it, moving to the triangle of curls between her thighs. She stiffened when he tasted her.

He raised his head slightly. "Open your legs."

She did as she was told. His mouth returned, his tongue probed. Sinking and withdrawing. Flicking the sensitive bud lightly. Finally, the sensations were too much. Heat surged through her, building until the pressure peaked and burst into a feeling of such intense pleasure, she cried out.

When it subsided, she found herself in Jake's arms. He cuddled her against him. Feeling closer to him than ever, she reached for him once again, but he stopped her before she could take him in her palm.

"I'd rather not," he croaked, knowing if she touched him he would explode. "We can talk again in a week. After you've seen the doctor."

She was both touched and surprised by the concern she saw in his eyes. "You're a nice man, Jake."

He grinned. "So, I've been trying to tell you for months."

She closed her fist around him despite his objections. "Which is why I'm not about to send you away in your condition."

Jake closed his eyes and gave in to her touch.

The room was light when Jake opened his eyes the next morning. He glanced at the alarm clock, and was startled to see it was after nine.

Then he realized it was Sunday and he didn't have to go in to work. He was thankful to be spared another day at the front desk.

He climbed from the bed and tiptoed to the nursery where he found Sammie nursing the baby. She smiled at the sight of him.

"Hi," she said.

"Hi yourself." The baby jumped at the sound of his voice. He walked over to the rocking chair and stroked the back of her head. "She's grown," he said.

"Her pediatrician is pleased with how she's doing."

"Don't you worry about her sleeping all the way over here?"

"I have a monitor on my night table. I can hear every sound she makes. But I'd much rather have her in a room next door. I should probably think of moving when my lease is up next month."

"You could move in with me."

She didn't answer. Instead, she sat Stephie up in her lap and patted her softly until she burped. Then she lay her on her stomach in the crib. "You want a cup of coffee?" she asked Jake as she crossed the room.

He pulled her in his arms and kissed her. "I'd love one."

Holding hands, they made their way into the kitchen where Sammie poured two cups of coffee and handed him one. "How'd you sleep?"

"Fine, considering."

"Considering what?"

"That I would have preferred making love to you all night."

She met his gaze and knew that he was sincere. It did her heart good to know she was still appealing after all the months she'd spent feeling like a balloon. She took his hand once more. "Let's sit in the living room."

They sat together on the sofa, Jake stretching his legs out on the coffee table. "What do you want to do today? I have the whole day."

"How about unpack my things?"

"Naw, I was thinking of something fun."

She took a sip of coffee, then shot him a sideways glance.

"What?"

"I heard you had a new job."

He frowned. "Who told you?"

"Marlene. She said she didn't know that much, only that it's a desk job and you're supposed to wear a suit and tie." She waited for him to say something, but he didn't. "Have you been promoted?"

He slipped his legs from the coffee table and sat up straight, placing his coffee cup before him. "No, it's not a promotion. I'm being punished for not following orders."

"Then it's only temporary?"

"You sound disappointed."

"I guess I am. I thought—"

"You thought I'd been transferred to another department, that maybe I'd requested it because of you?" When she glanced away, he pressed her. "Is that right? Is that why you invited me to stay last night?" He nudged her. "Look at me."

She faced him. "Yes."

He sighed and raked one hand through his hair. "Okay," he said wearily. "I'll do what I have to do to have you, Sammie. If this is what it takes to win your love, so be it."

She held her breath. "You mean you'll get out of narcotics?"

"Or anything else that smacks of danger. I'm tired of fighting you over what I do for a living. I'm tired of defending myself for doing what I feel serves some sort of purpose."

"You'd do that for me?"

"For us. We can't be together, can't be happy as long as you have to live in fear of something happening to me. The only thing that's likely to happen to me on this job is getting writer's cramp."

She threw her arms around him. "Thank you, Jake! I know you won't regret this decision."

She was literally grinning from ear to ear. "Then you'll marry me?" he asked.

She could not remember being happier. "Of course I'll marry you. We'll plan a small wedding with just our close friends."

"You're welcome to move to my place anytime you like." He sighed. "Well, I'd best get dressed." He pulled away and walked into the bedroom, grabbing his jeans and stepping into them. Sammie walked into the room as he was pulling on his shirt.

"Where are you going?"

He fumbled beneath the bed for his shoes. "Home. I've got a lot to do."

"I thought you wanted to go somewhere."

He paused in thought. "Maybe we should do it next weekend. I haven't paid my bills or mowed the grass in three weeks. I'll call you; maybe we'll do something later."

Sammie followed him to the door, and he kissed her briefly before leaving. She closed the door and leaned against it. He had made the sacrifice. He loved her enough to do whatever was necessary to make her happy. That was some kind of love.

So why did she suddenly feel uneasy?

FOURTEEN

Jake stepped through the front door to find his house decorated in balloons and streamers. He walked into the kitchen where Stephie looked up from her mechanical swing. When he saw Sammie in a short red dress with black net stockings and high heels, he gave a slow whistle.

"Hey there, big boy," she said, with a terrible Mae West impersonation.

"What's all this?"

"A celebration." She crossed the room, slipped her arms inside his suit coat, and kissed him hard on the mouth. "I went to the doctor today."

"And?"

She loosened his tie. "I'm healed."

This time he kissed her. He had moved her and the baby into his place at the beginning of the week, and he realized now how much he looked forward to coming home at the end of the day because of them. Ruby was in the process of planning the wedding; they were shooting for three weeks away. "That's good news," he said at last.

She went back to the stove. "So how was your day?" she asked a bit too brightly.

He shrugged. "Same as usual." He reached into the refrigerator and pulled out a beer, then turned toward the hall. "I'm going to get out of this monkey suit," he said, then disappeared.

Sammie wound up the baby swing and watched him go. Jake wasn't happy. Not that he'd said anything, but she could see the disappointment in his eyes, the absence of life. Not only that, he was drinking too much. Several beers a night, in fact, while he sat in front of the TV and thought about Lord only knew what. He'd fallen asleep on the sofa twice that week. He didn't care about going out or even talking to his friends when they called on the phone. It wasn't like him.

Did he wish she and Stephie had never moved in?

The thought frightened her. She had never been happier. The house was perfect, and there was a big backyard where Stephie could play one day, where her and Jake's children could play. With Jake beside her, she looked forward to getting up in the morning; she looked forward to life period. Now it would be even better since the doctor had given her a clean bill of health.

Jake was just overwhelmed at the moment, she told herself. He had a new job and new people living under his roof. That would overwhelm anybody.

Sammie turned the dinner on low, took the baby out of the swing and carried her to the back bedroom that was serving as the nursery. Jake had already told her she could decorate the house anyway she liked, and she looked forward to doing just that. She changed the baby and nursed her until she fell asleep, then put her in the crib and tiptoed out of the room, closing the door softly behind her.

Sammie noted Jake hadn't come out of their room yet. When she opened the door, he was sprawled across the bed in his underwear, sound asleep. She walked over to the bed and sat down, then studied his face for a moment as he slept. She couldn't remember at what point she'd fallen in love with him, only that she had. She couldn't recall when she'd begun to need him, only that she did. She wanted to spend the rest of her life with him, without fear of having him snatched away. Everything she'd ever cared for in her life had been taken away from her. Her parents. Nathan.

She was determined now to protect the people she loved the most—Jake and Stephie. She was not going to let anything happen to either of them.

"Hey, why the serious face?"

Sammie jumped at the sound of his voice. She looked down and found Jake watching her. "I thought you were asleep."

He grabbed her arm and pulled her down beside him. "How can I sleep when you're sitting there looking so damn sexy and smelling so good?"

She started to respond, but he covered her mouth with his own. It was a hungry kiss, greedy. He slid one hand up her thigh, beneath her dress. As he undressed her, he kissed each spot he bared until she sighed her immense pleasure. When he entered her, they both cried out from intensity. Their bodies, it seemed, had been designed for each other. Their souls harmonized, entwining their hearts and emotions forever. Their orgasms were simultaneous and earth-shattering.

Afterward Sammie lay in the crook of his arm, gazing at the ceiling. "I'd almost forgotten what it was like," she confessed, then chuckled softly. "But then, it was never like *that*."

It was on the tip of his tongue to tell her it had been the same for him, but he was still dealing with the emotions their lovemaking had stirred inside of him; emotions that had become calloused and hard over the years because of his job. He pulled her closer. "I take it that's supposed to be a compliment?" he said.

"Darn right it is. Makes me wonder why we waited so long."

"If I remember correctly, you were pregnant."

They were silent for a moment.

"Can we talk?" she finally asked.

He turned over onto his side and propped himself up on one elbow. "This sounds serious. What is it?"

"Are you happy with Stephie and me being here?"

"Of course I am. It's what I've wanted all along."

"You seem different somehow. Is it your new job?"

He lowered his head and kissed her softly. "It takes some getting used to, Sammie. I'll be okay. What smells so good?"

He was changing the subject. "Chicken and rice casserole. You hungry?"

He nodded and reached for his clothes. "Starved."

Sammie put on a pair of cutoffs and a T-shirt. "Ruby called today," she said. "She found the perfect place for us to be married. It's a little open-air chapel north of here that overlooks the lake. She wants us to see it. I told her we might drive up Sunday. What do you think?"

"Sounds good. Did you tell her I wanted the baby to be in the wedding too?"

Sammie smiled. "Yes. We're looking for a dress."

He followed her down the hall, pinching her playfully on the rear. "You don't need a new dress," he said. "You've got that red thing and those black stockings."

She chuckled and jumped as he goosed her. This was the Jake she knew and loved. "Of course! Why didn't *I* think of that?"

Jake had barely settled himself behind his desk when his phone rang. It was the captain. "Be in my office in ten minutes," he ordered and hung up.

Jake made his way to the second floor a few minutes later and stepped into the narcotics department. He was instantly assaulted by wolf whistles from his colleagues.

"You look good in a suit, Flannery," one of the men said. "Does it have to be dry-cleaned or can you just toss it in the wash with everything else you own?"

He was used to the teasing by now. "Very funny. At least I own a suit, which is more than I can say for you slugs." He paused at the captain's door and knocked.

"Why does he want to see you?" another asked.

Jake shrugged. "Beats the hell out of me."

Captain Mitchell answered the door, saw the other men staring and eyed them sharply. "Don't ya'll have something to do?" They jumped and went back to work. He almost slammed the door once Jake walked through. "Sit down, Flannery," he ordered and made his way around his desk to his chair. "Nice suit."

"Thanks." Jake said as he sat down.

The other man folded his hands in front of him. "So, how's the new job working out?"

Jake wondered if the captain was making fun of him. How did he think the job was working out? It was boring as hell. Jake decided he wouldn't give him the satisfaction of admitting that. "I'm doing what I'm getting paid for," he said.

The captain leaned back in his chair and looked at him. "You know what your problem is, Flannery? You're too damn cocky. You've always been that way. I remember when you were fresh out of the academy. You thought you were top dog even then. I was thankful you weren't in my unit at the time. But then, I started hearing great things about you. You developed one hell of a reputation.

"I didn't know whether to laugh or cry when you got transferred over here, but I soon found out, cocky or not, you knew your business. You're the best man I've ever had, Jake."

"Thanks, Captain," he said aloud. "That certainly explains why I'm answering phones."

"Don't get smart with me, Flannery, or I'll send you to the mailroom next." He paused and sighed. "You're still cocky, and you don't always follow the rules." He leaned forward as though he were about to share a secret. "See, we can't protect you if we don't know what you're doing. But I don't have to tell you that, do I? You've been around almost as long as I have. You'll probably end up with my job before it's over.

"I can't let the rest of those dodo heads out there think they can go off half-cocked like you do. They'll end up dead."

"So you put me on the desk to make an example out of me," Jake said.

"And I'll probably end up doing it once or twice again before I retire. But right now, I want you back in narcotics. We got some things coming down in the next couple of weeks. I can't send these guys out there without you." He paused. "But before you come back, I want you to promise that you'll work with me. I don't want any more surprises. Take the weekend to think about it. I'll expect you back in here Monday morning."

Jake sat there for a moment, not quite knowing what to say. Mitchell shuffled papers on his desk, and Jake knew he'd been dismissed. He stood and made his way to the door. "Thanks, Captain."

❧————————❧

The chapel was small, perched on a knoll, overlooking Lake Lanier. Although the building itself was very rustic and would only accommodate twenty-five or thirty people, Sammie thought it was perfect.

Ruby watched Sammie and Jake carefully. "I had no idea it was so . . . primitive," she said. "Maybe it's not what you want after all."

Sammie turned to Jake. "What do you think, honey?" she asked. Jake had been quiet on the ride up. In fact, he hadn't said more than a handful of words in two days.

"Huh?" Jake glanced up.

"Jake, are you even listening to me?" Sammie said, smiling in an attempt to hide her worry.

"No, I wasn't," he admitted. "I guess I'm not really into planning weddings. Why don't you decide. You know I'll go along with whatever you say. I always do, don't I?"

The last comment was like a slap in the face to Sammie. She and Ruby exchanged nervous looks. "Ruby, would you take the baby out to the car for a moment?" she said, handing her the infant. "I'd like to speak with Jake."

The older woman nodded and took the baby, then left the chapel. Sammie didn't waste any time. "What's going on, Jake?" she demanded.

"You've been acting weird for days. I can't take it anymore."

Jake sat down on the first pew and continued to gaze at the water. "Do you have any idea how much I love you, Sammie?" he said, almost as though he were talking to himself.

"Well, I hope you don't mind my pointing out that you have a strange way of showing it. You don't even talk to me anymore."

He extended his arm. "Come, sit by me."

Sammie had a strange, sinking sensation that he was about to give her bad news. She walked over to him and sat down. "What?"

He raised her hand to his lips and kissed her palm. He gazed at her for a long moment. "This isn't going to work, babe."

Her stomach clenched tightly at his words. It wasn't going to work. She should have known. Nothing ever lasted for very long. Her own parents had abandoned her when she was just four days old. "You mean us getting married?" she asked, her voice trembling.

"I would gladly marry you today," he said. "You don't know what it's meant to me to have you and Stephie. The problem is with me. I can't be the man you want me to be."

"It's your job," she said, her tone flat. "It always comes back to that."

"The captain has decided I've been punished enough. He wants me back in narcotics on Monday."

Her eyes misted. She should have known. "Oh, this is great," she said.

"If I stayed at this desk job, I'd come to resent you for asking me to. And that resentment would turn to hate. We don't need that, and neither does your daughter. I love you too much to let it happen."

Sammie ignored him. "I'll have to get my things out of your house."

"I'll help you."

"I don't want your help."

"You and Ruby can't do it alone."

"Why the hell do you care *how* I do it?"

He grabbed her by the shoulders and stared into her eyes. "Because I still love you, dammit, and I'm not going to have you hurting yourself. I said I'll do it."

She was openly crying now. "Call the apartment before you come by. I'd rather not be there." She clutched her purse to her and started for the door. "I'll ride back with Ruby."

FIFTEEN

Sammie cried all the way back to Ruby's house, and matters were made even worse when Stephie picked that particular time to be fussy. No amount of bouncing would soothe her.

"She knows you're upset," Ruby said, glancing over at Sammie. "Babies can sense it right away."

They arrived at Ruby's house, and Sammie put the baby to sleep on a bed in the guest room, positioning several pillows around her for safety's sake. Ruby peeked her head inside the door.

"I've made fresh coffee," she announced. "Come have a cup, and let's talk."

Sammie was thankful Ruby's husband was taking a nap. As she sipped her coffee, she tried to get her emotions under control. "And to think

I assumed childbirth was the most painful thing I would have to go through in life. I was wrong."

"Do you want to talk about it?" Ruby asked.

Sammie propped an elbow on the table and leaned her head on her hand. "It all boils down to his job, Ruby. He doesn't want to give it up."

Ruby gazed at her. "I suspected as much." She paused and looked thoughtful for a moment. "What are you afraid of, Sammie?"

Sammie looked at her. "You shouldn't have to ask me that. You saw what I went through after Nathan was killed."

Ruby took her hand. "Honey, Jake has been with the department for fifteen years. He's no rookie. We both know Nathan was a hothead. He wasn't always careful. How many times have I heard you say you didn't know what Nathan was doing on the police force?" She squeezed her hand. "You ask me, Jake was born to be a cop."

"I appreciate what you're trying to do, Ruby," Sammie said. "But it's not going to work. I am not going through that again. I refuse to marry Jake and then end up losing him just like I've lost everybody else I've ever loved. I won't do it."

Ruby sat there for a moment. "Seems to me you lose no matter which way you go."

Sammie realized with a sinking heart that it was true.

Ruby insisted Sammie spend the night. The

two women cooked dinner—chicken fried steak
with mashed potatoes and gravy—while Ruby's
husband, Bill, played with the baby in front of
the television set. As Ruby stirred the gravy,
Sammie peered over her shoulder doubtfully.

"I don't know, Ruby. Looks like there might
be five zillion calories in there."

Ruby chuckled. "It won't hurt for you to go
off your diet for one night," she said. "Besides,
Bill and I have an agreement. If he keeps to his
diet without grumbling or cheating, I prepare
something a little sinful now and then. It's the
only way I can coax him into eating right."

"Well, whatever works," Sammie said, rubbing her tired eyes. She had cried until they were
itchy and swollen. Now she was doing her best
to remain cheerful. She had decided she would
go home the next day and get her things in order
so she could start back to work on Tuesday. Otherwise she would just sit around feeling sorry for
herself.

With dinner ready, Sammie lay the baby on a
blanket nearby and joined Ruby and Bill at the
table. Once Bill said grace, they began to pass
bowls back and forth to one another, dishing the
food onto their plates. Although Sammie wasn't
really hungry, she took a little of everything and
exclaimed to Ruby how good it was.

Bill's nap had revived him and put him in
good spirits. He told off-color jokes and several
funny stories about friends throughout dinner.

Before long, Sammie found herself laughing right along with him.

"Does he always do this?" she asked Ruby, glancing at her. Bill was laughing so hard, he was wheezing.

Ruby rolled her eyes and nodded. "He always has something funny to say. You should see him when our kids visit." She looked at her husband and frowned. "Bill, take a break from the jokes already. Your face is turning blue."

Sammie glanced at the man and felt her smile freeze on her face. "Bill?" She saw the purplish tint to his face, the bulging eyes. Panic gripped her. "Oh my God, he's choking!" she cried. She toppled her chair as she rose from the table.

Ruby was beside her in an instant. "We've got to do something! Call nine-one-one."

"Get up, Bill!" Sammie said, tugging him. He seemed not to hear. "Help me get him up," she told Ruby.

The next few minutes seemed to drag. They struggled for a moment. Finally, Bill was standing. Sammie hadn't realized what a big man he was. Moving quickly, she got behind him and wrapped her arms around his waist. His face was a dangerous-looking purple. She made a fist with one hand and grasped it with the other, then pulled back as hard as she could into his abdomen. Nothing happened.

"I'm calling an ambulance," Ruby said, racing into the kitchen.

Sammie tried again, a quick upward thrust. She could hear Ruby on the phone, sounding like she was about to lose it.

Sammie thought she might lose it as well. "Come on, Bill," she cried, jerking with all her might. She heard a gagging, coughing sound. "Bill?" she said frantically.

"It's out," he managed, then slumped, trembling, into his chair.

The paramedics arrived in record time and insisted on checking Bill out even though he told them he was okay.

"We're the ones they should be checking," Ruby whispered to Sammie, still very much shaken. "I think I almost had a heart attack. Thank God you knew what to do. He would have been dead by now had I been alone." As though suddenly realizing how close she'd come to losing her husband, she started to cry.

Sammie took the older woman in her arms. "It's okay, Ruby," she said, her own voice choked with emotion. "Bill is fine now."

"You saved his life," the tearful woman said. "You saved my husband's life."

Bill saw the paramedics to the door, then put his arm around his wife's shoulders. "You need to lie down for a few minutes." He led her toward the hall, then glanced over his shoulder at Sammie and winked. "Thanks. I owe you one."

Sammie had cleaned the kitchen, and bathed and fed Stephie by the time Ruby appeared in her bathrobe. "I took a little nap, then stood under a hot shower for a while," the woman said. "It calmed my nerves." She glanced at the clean kitchen. "I know Bill didn't do that."

Sammie smiled. "Would you like something to drink?"

"No. I just want to sit on the screened porch for a while. Come sit with me?"

"Sure." Sammie followed her. "I didn't think I'd ever get Stephie to sleep."

Ruby pushed through a glass door leading to the porch. "All that excitement had her stirred up." She took a seat in one of the chairs that overlooked a perfectly manicured backyard. She was quiet for a moment. "Bill's choking made me think of something, Sammie," she said at last.

Sammie could see that her friend was still shaken over the incident. She took her hand and squeezed it. "What?"

"You know how worried you've been about how dangerous Jake's job is?" When Sammie nodded, she went on. "Well, just think. I almost lost my husband while he was sitting at the kitchen table." She looked at Sammie. "The way I see it, it doesn't matter if you're eating dinner or in the middle of a drug raid. When it's your time to go, there's not a dang thing you can do about it. Except make the best of life while you're here."

Sammie pondered it. "I guess I never thought about it that way."

By the time Sammie returned home the following day, Jake had delivered her things. She straightened the house, put in a load of wash, and thought again about what Ruby had said the night before.

The apartment was lonely. She missed Jake. Jake, her best friend. Jake, her lover. How would she get through life without him? How would she even make it through one more night? She picked up the telephone to call him, then put it down. He still had a dangerous job. If something happened to him, she would be devastated. But she would lose him forever anyway if she didn't take that one risk. Jake was smart and cautious. Levelheaded. She had trusted him with her heart. She had trusted him enough to need him when she'd promised herself she'd never need anybody. Now she had to trust him enough to take care of himself.

He smelled her perfume even before he saw the red dress lying on the floor. Jake frowned as he closed the front door, walked over to the flimsy garment, and picked it up. He put it to his nose and glanced around the room for some clue as to what was going on. A pair of black net stockings was draped over a lamp shade.

He started down the hall. It was quiet. The door to the guest room was ajar. He saw the baby sleeping on the bed, and closed the door softly before walking to his bedroom. A pair of sheer panties were draped over the doorknob. He plucked them off and went in.

He found her in the large garden tub in his bathroom, soaking in suds to her chin. He crossed his arms and leaned against the door. She smiled when she saw him.

"Hello, handsome," she said, noting how much better he looked in his jeans and blazer than the suit.

"Haven't I told you a hundred times not to leave your clothes all over the place?" he asked, holding up the panties. "What's going on, Sammie?"

"I've decided to move back in."

He arched one black brow in surprise and moved to the tub where he sat on the edge. "What changed your mind?"

She didn't hesitate. "Me. I love you too much to give you up, Jake. I was so worried about losing you that I didn't realize I would lose you anyway if I didn't take this risk."

He reached over and fingered a tendril of

hair that rested against her cheek. "I don't want my job coming between us," he said softly.

She met his gaze. "It won't. As long as you promise me here and now that you'll act responsibly. I don't want you taking unnecessary chances. If I didn't already know how good you are—the best in the business—I wouldn't be making this deal."

"You've been talking to the captain?" he asked.

"We had lunch together one day this week. I told him my concerns. He was very reassuring."

He studied her. Her cheeks were flushed from the warm water. Although the suds covered her, he spied one rosy nipple peeking out. "So, does this mean we can get married after all?" he asked hopefully.

"If you still want to."

"Dumb question," he said, standing and shrugging off his coat. He hung it on a hook on the back of the door. "Of course I do." He turned, his hands on his hips. "How long—?"

Sammie grinned. "She'll sleep for a couple of hours."

"Good." He leaned over, thrust his arms into the water and scooped her up.

She squealed. "What are you doing?"

"Taking you to bed."

"I'm all wet," she said, noting she was getting him wet as well.

"Minor detail." He paused. "Grab that towel."

In the bedroom he lay her down gently and dried her with the fluffy bath towel. Her skin was as pink and soft as Stephie's. "You're beautiful," he said. "Don't ever leave me again."

She saw the dark warning in his eyes as she slid her arms around his neck and pulled him down for a kiss. "I promise."

He kissed her deeply, hungrily. When he raised his head, his eyes were serious. "I want to be married right away," he said. "And I want to start adoption proceedings on the baby. I don't want Stephie growing up without a father."

Sammie reached for the buttons on his shirt. "You're a good man, Jake," she said softly.

He grinned and helped her peel off the shirt. "Give me a few minutes, and I'll show you just how good."

She pulled his head down for another kiss.

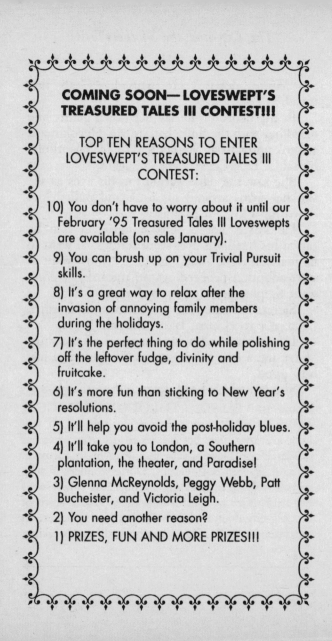

THE EDITOR'S CORNER

What better way to celebrate the holidays than with four terrific new LOVESWEPTs! And this month we are excited to present you with romances that are full of passion, humor, and most of all, true love—everything that is best about this time of year. So sit back and indulge yourself in the magic of the season.

Starting things off is the fabulous Mary Kay McComas with **PASSING THROUGH MIDNIGHT**, LOVESWEPT #722. Gil Howlett believes all women are mysteries, but he *has* to discover what has driven Dorie Devries into hiding in his hometown! Struggling with old demons, Dorie wonders if deep sorrow ever heals, but Gil's tenderness slowly wins her trust. Now he must soothe the wounded spirit of this big-city doctor who challenges him to believe in forgotten dreams. Heartwarming and heartbreaking,

Mary Kay's novels weave a marvelous tapestry of emotions into stories you wish would never end.

The wonderfully talented Debra Dixon wants to introduce you to **DOC HOLIDAY**, LOVESWEPT #723. Drew Haywood needs an enchantress to help give his son a holiday to remember—and no one does Christmas better than Taylor Bishop! She can transform a house into a home that smells of gingerbread and sparkles with tinsel, and kissing her is like coming out of the cold. She's spent her whole life caring for others, but when sweet temptation beckons, this sexy family man must convince her to break all her rules. With poignant humor and sizzling sensuality, Debra has crafted an unforgettable story of the magic of Christmas.

The ever-popular Adrienne Staff returns with **SPELLBOUND**, LOVESWEPT #724. Edward Rockford sees her first in the shadows and senses the pretty artist somehow holds the key to his secrets—but when he enters Jamie Payton's loft, he is stunned to discover that her painting reveals what he's hidden from all the world. Haunted by ghosts from the past, Jamie yearns to share his sanctuary. But can his seductive sorcery set her free? Conjured of equal parts destiny and mystery, passion and emotion, Adrienne's stories capture the imagination and compel the heart to believe once more in a love for all time.

Last but never least is Susan Connell with **RINGS ON HER FINGERS**, LOVESWEPT #725. She really knows how to fill her Christmas stockings, Steve Stratton decides with admiration at first sight of the long-legged brunette dressed as a holiday elf! Gwen Mansfield feels her heart racing like a runaway sleigh when the gorgeous architect invites her to play under his tree—and vows to be good. A jinxed love life has made her wary, but maybe Steve is the one to change her luck. Susan Connell has always written about intrepid heroes and damsels in just enough distress to make life interesting, but now she delivers the perfect Christmas present, complete with surprises and glittering fun!

Happy reading!

With best wishes,

Beth de Guzman

Senior Editor

P.S. Don't miss the exciting women's novels that are coming your way from Bantam in January! **HEAVEN'S PRICE,** from blockbuster author Sandra Brown, is a classic romantic novel in hardcover for the first time; **LORD OF ENCHANTMENT,** by bestselling author Suzanne Robinson, is an enchanting tale of romance and intrigue on a stormy isle off the coast of Elizabethan England; **SURRENDER TO A STRANGER,** by Karyn Monk, is an utterly compelling, passionately romantic debut from an exceptionally talented new historical romance author. We'll be giving you a sneak peek at these terrific books in next month's LOVESWEPTs. And immediately following this page look for a preview of the exciting romances from Bantam that are *available now!*

Don't miss these sensational books by
your favorite Bantam authors

On sale in November

ADAM'S FALL
by Sandra Brown

PURE SIN
by Susan Johnson

ON WINGS OF MAGIC
by Kay Hooper

ADAM'S FALL

by

SANDRA BROWN

"Ms. Brown's larger than life heroes and heroines
make you believe all the warm, wonderful,
wild things in life."
—*Rendezvous*

BLOCKBUSTER AUTHOR SANDRA BROWN—
WHOSE NAME IS ALMOST SYNONYMOUS
WITH *THE NEW YORK TIMES* BEST-
SELLER LIST—OFFERS A CLASSIC ROMAN-
TIC NOVEL THAT ACHES WITH EMOTION
AND SIZZLES WITH PASSION. . . .

They still fought like cats and dogs, but their relationship drastically improved.

He still cursed her, accused her of being heartless
out of pure meanness, and insisted that she pushed
him beyond his threshold of pain and endurance.

She still cursed him and accused him of being a

gutless rich kid who, for the first time in his charmed life, was experiencing hardship.

He said she couldn't handle patients worth a damn.

She said he couldn't handle adversity worth a damn.

He said she taunted him unmercifully.

She said he whined incessantly.

And so it went. But things were definitely better. He came to trust her just a little. He began to listen when she told him that he wasn't trying hard enough and should put more concentration into it. And he listened when she advised that he was trying too hard and needed to rest awhile.

"Didn't I tell you so?" She was standing at the foot of his bed, giving therapy to his ankle.

"I'm still not ready to tap dance."

"But you've got sensation."

"You stuck a straight pin into my big toe!"

"But you've got sensation." She stopped turning his foot and looked up toward the head of his bed, demanding that he agree.

"I've got sensation." The admission was grumbled, but he couldn't hide his pleased smile.

"In only two and a half weeks." She whistled. "You've come a long way, baby. I'm calling Honolulu today and ordering a set of parallel bars. You'll soon be able to stand between them."

His smile collapsed. "I'll never be able to do that."

"That's what you said about the wheelchair. Will you lighten up?"

"Will you?" He grunted with pain as she bent his knee back toward his chest.

"Not until you're walking."

"If you keep wearing those shorts, I'll soon be running. I'll be chasing you."

"Promises, promises."

"I thought I told you to dress more modestly."

"This is Hawaii, Cavanaugh. Everybody goes casual, or haven't you heard? I'm going to resist the movement now. Push against my hand. That's it. A little harder. Good."

"Ah, God," he gasped through clenched teeth. He followed her instructions, which took him through a routine to stretch his calf muscle. "The backs of your legs are sunburned," he observed as he put forth even greater effort.

"You noticed?"

"How could I help it? You flash them by me every chance you get. Think those legs of yours are long enough? They must start in your armpits. But how'd I get off on that? What were we talking about?"

"Why my legs were sunburned. Okay, Adam, let up a bit, then try it again. Come on now, no ugly faces. One more time." She picked up the asinine conversation in order to keep his mind off his discomfort. "My legs are sunburned because I fell asleep beside the pool yesterday afternoon."

"Is that what you're being paid an exorbitant amount of money to do? To nap beside my swimming pool?"

"Of course not!" After a strategic pause, she added, "I went swimming too." He gave her a baleful look and pressed his foot against the palm of her hand. "Good, Adam, good. Once more."

"You said that was the last one."

"I lied."

"You heartless bitch."

"You gutless preppy."

Things were swell.

"Susan Johnson brings sensuality to new heights
and beyond."
—*Romantic Times*

Susan Johnson

NATIONALLY BESTSELLING AUTHOR
OF *SEIZED BY LOVE* AND *OUTLAW*

PURE SIN

*From the erotic imagination of bestselling author Susan
Johnson comes a tale of exquisite pleasure that begins in the
wilds of Montana—and ends in the untamed places of two
lovers' hearts.*

"A shame we didn't ever meet," Adam said with a
seductive smile, his responses automatic with beautiful women. "Good conversation is rare."

She didn't suppose most women were interested
exclusively in his conversation, Flora thought, as she
took in the full splendor of his dark beauty and
power. Even lounging in a chair, his legs casually
crossed at the ankles, he presented an irresistible image of brute strength. And she'd heard enough rumor
in the course of the evening to understand he enjoyed
women—nonconversationally. "As rare as marital fi-
delity no doubt."

His brows rose fractionally. "No one's had the
nerve to so bluntly allude to my marriage. Are you

speaking of Isolde's or my infidelities?" His grin was boyish.

"Papa says you're French."

"Does that give me motive or excuse? And I'm only half French, as you no doubt know, so I may have less excuse than Isolde. She apparently prefers Baron Lacretelle's properties in Paris and Nice to my dwelling here."

"No heartbroken melancholy?"

He laughed. "Obviously you haven't met Isolde."

"Why did you marry then?"

He gazed at her for a moment over the rim of the goblet he'd raised to his lips. "You can't be that naive," he softly said, then quickly drained the glass.

"Forgive me. I'm sure it's none of my business."

"I'm sure it's not." The warmth had gone from his voice and his eyes. Remembering the reason he'd married Isolde always brought a sense of chaffing anger.

"I haven't felt so gauche in years," Flora said, her voice almost a whisper.

His black eyes held hers, their vital energy almost mesmerizing, then his look went shuttered and his grin reappeared. "How could you know, darling? About the idiosyncrasies of my marriage. Tell me now about your first sight of Hagia Sophia."

"It was early in the morning," she began, relieved he'd so graciously overlooked her faux pas. "The sun had just begun to appear over the crest of the—"

"Come dance with me," Adam abruptly said, leaning forward in his chair. "This waltz is a favorite of mine," he went on, as though they hadn't been discussing something completely different. Reaching over, he took her hands in his. "And I've been wanting to"—his hesitation was minute as he discarded the inappropriate verb—"hold you." He grinned. "You see how blandly circumspect my choice of words is." Rising, he gently pulled her to her feet. "Considering the newest scandal in my life, I'm on my best behavior tonight."

"But then scandals don't bother me." She was standing very close to him, her hands still twined in his.

His fine mouth, only inches away, was graced with a genial smile and touched with a small heated playfulness. "I thought they might not."

"When one travels as I do, one becomes inured to other people's notions of nicety." Her bare shoulders lifted briefly, ruffling the limpid lace on her décolletage. He noticed both the pale satin of her skin and the tantalizing swell of her bosom beneath the delicate lace. "If I worried about scandal," she murmured with a small smile, "I'd never set foot outside England."

"And you do."

"Oh yes," she whispered. And for a moment both were speaking of something quite different.

"You're not helping," he said in a very low voice. "I've sworn off women for the moment."

"To let your wounds heal?"

"Nothing so poetical." His quirked grin reminded her of a teasing young boy. "I'm reassessing my priorities."

"Did I arrive in Virginia City too late then?"

"Too late?" One dark brow arched infinitesimally.

"To take advantage of your former priorities."

He took a deep breath because he was already perversely aware of the closeness of her heated body, of the heady fragrance of her skin. "You're a bold young lady, Miss Bonham."

"I'm twenty-six years old, Mr. Serre, and independent."

"I'm not sure after marriage to Isolde that I'm interested in any more willful aristocratic ladies."

"Perhaps I could change your mind."

He thoughtfully gazed down at her, and then the faintest smile lifted the graceful curve of his mouth. "Perhaps you could."

Kay Hooper

NATIONALLY BESTSELLING AUTHOR OF
THE WIZARD OF SEATTLE

ON WINGS OF MAGIC

*One of today's most beloved romance authors, Kay Hooper
captivates readers with the wit and sensuality of her work.
Now the award-winning writer offers a passionate story
filled with all the humor and tenderness her fans have
come to expect—a story that explores the loneliness of
heartbreak and the searing power of love. . . .*

"Tell me, Kendall—why the charade?"

"Why not?" She looked at him wryly. "I am what
people expect me to be."

"You mean men."

"Sure. Oh, I could rant and rave about not being
valued for who I am instead of what I look like, but
what good would that do? My way is much easier.
And there's no harm done."

"I don't know about that." Seriously, he went on,
"By being what people expect you to be, you don't
give anyone the chance to see the real you."

Interested in spite of herself, she frowned thoughtfully. "But how many people really care what's beneath the surface, Hawke? Not many," she went on, answering her own question. "We all act out roles we've given ourselves, pretend to be things we're not—or things we want to be. And we build walls around the things we want to hide."

"What do you want to hide, Kendall?" he asked softly.

Ignoring the question, she continued calmly. "It's human nature. We want to guess everyone else's secrets without giving our own away."

"And if someone wants to see beneath the surface?"

Kendall shrugged. "We make them dig for it. You know—make them prove themselves worthy of our trust. Of all the animals on this earth, we're the most suspicious of a hand held out in friendship."

Hawke pushed his bowl away and gazed at her with an oddly sober gleam in his eyes. "Sounds like you learned that lesson the hard way," he commented quietly.

She stared at him, surprise in her eyes, realizing for the first time just how cynical she'd become. Obeying some nameless command in his smoky eyes, she said slowly, "I've seen too much to be innocent, Hawke. Whatever ideals I had . . . died long ago."

He stared at her for a long moment, then murmured, "I think I'd better find a pick and a shovel."

Suddenly angry with her own burst of self-revelation, Kendall snapped irritably, "Why?"

"To dig beneath the surface." He smiled slowly. "You're a fascinating lady, Kendall James. And I think

. . . if I dig deep enough . . . I just might find gold."

"What you might find," she warned coolly, "is a booby trap. I'm not a puzzle to be solved, Hawke."

"Aren't you? You act the sweet innocent, telling yourself that it's the easy way. And it's a good act, very convincing and probably very useful. But it isn't entirely an act, is it, honey? There is an innocent inside of you, hiding from the things she's seen."

"You're not a psychologist and I'm not a patient, so stop with the analyzing," she muttered, trying to ignore what he was saying.

"You're a romantic, an idealist," he went on as if she hadn't spoken. "But you hide that part of your nature—behind a wall that isn't a wall at all. You've got yourself convinced that it's an act, and that conviction keeps you from being hurt."

Kendall shot him a glare from beneath her lashes. "Now you're not even making sense," she retorted scornfully.

"Oh, yes, I am." His eyes got that hooded look she was beginning to recognize out of sheer self-defense. "A piece of the puzzle just fell into place. But it's still a long way from being solved. And, rest assured, Kendall, I intend to solve it."

"Is this in the nature of another warning?" she asked lightly, irritated that her heart had begun to beat like a jungle drum.

"Call it anything you like."

"I could just leave, you know."

"You could." The heavy lids lifted, revealing a cool challenge. "But that would be cowardly."

Knowing—*knowing*—that she was walking right

into his trap, Kendall snapped, "I'm a lot of things, Hawke, but a coward isn't one of them!" And felt strongly tempted to throw her soup bowl at him when she saw the satisfaction that flickered briefly in his eyes.

"Good," he said briskly. "Then we can forget about that angle, can't we? And get down to business."

"Business?" she murmured wryly. "That's one I haven't heard."

"Well, I would have called it romance, but I didn't want you to laugh at me." He grinned faintly. "Men are more romantic than women, you know. I read it somewhere."

"Fancy that." Kendall stared at him. "Most of the men I've known let romance go by the board."

"Really? Then knowing me will be an education."

And don't miss these wonderful romances from Bantam Books, on sale in December:

HEAVEN'S PRICE

by the *New York Times* bestselling author

Sandra Brown

a new hardcover edition of the Sandra Brown classic!

LORD OF ENCHANTMENT

by the nationally bestselling

Suzanne Robinson

"An author with star quality . . . spectacularly talented."
—*Romantic Times*

SURRENDER TO A STRANGER

by the highly talented

Karyn Monk

When a stranger risks everything to rescue a proud beauty, she owes him her life, her heart—and her soul. . . .

Don't miss these fabulous Bantam women's fiction titles

Now On Sale

ADAM'S FALL
by *New York Times* bestselling author
Sandra Brown

Blockbuster author Sandra Brown—whose name is almost synonymous with the *New York Times* bestseller list—offers a classic romantic novel that aches with emotion and sizzles with passion.
❏ *56768-3 $4.99/$5.99 in Canada*

PURE SIN
by nationally bestselling author
Susan Johnson

From the erotic imagination of Susan Johnson comes a tale of exquisite pleasure that begins in the wilds of Montana—and ends in the untamed places of two lovers' hearts.
❏ *29956-5 $5.50/6.99 in Canada*

ON WINGS OF MAGIC
by award-winning author
Kay Hooper

Award-winning Kay Hooper offers a passionate story filled with all the humor and tenderness her fans have come to expect—a story that explores the loneliness of heartbreak and the searing power of love.
❏ *56965-1 $4.99/$5.99 in Canada*